TENTACLE
&
WING

TENTACLE & WING

SARAH PORTER

HOUGHTON MIFFLIN HARCOURT
BOSTON NEW YORK

www.hmhco.com

Text set in 12 pt. Spectrum MT Std
Design by Christine Kettner

Library of Congress Cataloging-in-Publication Data
Names: Porter, Sarah, 1969- author.
Title: Tentacle and wing / Sarah Porter.
Description: Boston ; New York : Houghton Mifflin Harcourt, 2017. | Summary:
"Twelve-year-old Ada is a Chimera, one of a number of children born with human and
animal DNA thanks to a genetic experiment gone wrong. When she is shipped off to
a quarantined school for other kids like herself, she senses that the facility is keeping
a secret, which, if discovered, could upend everything the world knows about how
Chimeras came into being." — Provided by publisher.
Identifiers: LCCN 2016058460 | ISBN 9781328707338 (hardback)
Subjects: | CYAC: Genetic engineering — Fiction. | Quarantine — Fiction. |
Prejudices — Fiction. | Schools — Fiction. | Secrets — Fiction. | Racially mixed
people — Fiction. | Science fiction. | BISAC: JUVENILE FICTION / Family / Orphans
& Foster Homes. | JUVENILE FICTION / Science Fiction. | JUVENILE FICTION
/ Social Issues / Prejudice & Racism. | JUVENILE FICTION / Nature & the Natural
World / General (see also headings under Animals).
| JUVENILE FICTION / Social Issues / Self-Esteem & Self-Reliance. |
JUVENILE FICTION / Fantasy & Magic.
Classification: LCC PZ7.P8303 Ten 2017 | DDC [Fic] — dc23
LC record available at https://lccn.loc.gov/2016058460

Manufactured in the United States of America
DOC 10 9 8 7 6 5 4 3 2 1
4500673296

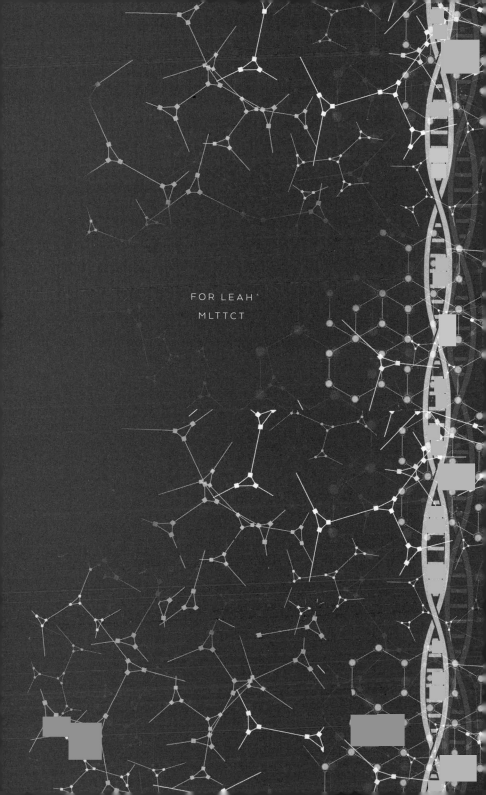

FOR LEAH
MLTTCT

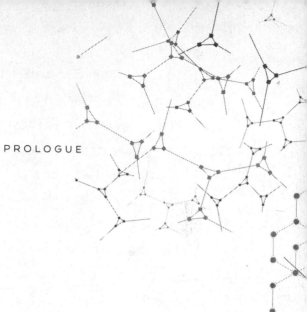

THE MOMENT Ada ran into the room, she noticed it: a soft ruby glow fuzzing through the dropped newspaper on the sofa, like the red smears left at the end of sunset.

"Ugh," her father said. "I put my glasses down two seconds ago . . . I was just holding them . . ." He twisted around, his mouth pursed in confusion, and Ada laughed. He was looking right at them!

"There, Daddy!"

"Where?" The glow was dimmer now, starting to fade out, but it was still obvious. She could hardly believe he didn't see it.

"Right there!" She flicked the newspaper aside. Silver frames gleamed against the flowered cushions.

He looked at her, startled. "How did you know? You weren't in the room when I put them down, were you?"

How could he ask such a silly question? She shook her

head hard, baffled at having to explain, and her black pigtails swung out like wings. "I saw them!"

"You saw them. Through the newspaper?" He shoved his glasses on at a haphazard angle and stared at her through the winking lenses. "Are you sure?"

"I saw the glow where things are warm," Ada told him. Her voice squeaked with impatience. "The red glow!"

He looked from her to the newspaper and back again, his brows pinched together. Then he lifted the paper and let it hang down like a curtain with his other hand hidden behind it. "Ada, sweetheart. This might be serious. How many fingers am I holding up?"

It seemed like a stupid game; she'd known how to count for years. He must realize that. The cloudy shape shone clearly through the paper. But she'd play if he wanted her to.

"Three."

"And now?"

"One finger."

"And now?"

"No fingers! You're making a fist."

He'd started nodding vigorously to himself. "Infrared vision. It *has* to be. And there might be more. Oh, God. We've been so focused on studying the obvious ones that we never even thought to *check*—But of course, of course there might be variations that aren't visible!" The words didn't make any sense to her, and she was getting bored. She wandered to the window and he followed, then knelt beside her and put his arm around her shoulder. They both looked out on a sky of flat, featureless blue above the shingled houses lining the street. "Ada? Can you describe the sky for me? Try to tell me exactly what you see."

Another crazy question. Why should she describe it when he could see it too? If Ada hadn't loved him so much, she might have turned sullen and refused to keep playing. "It's like peacocks."

"Peacocks?"

"Like a million peacocks with big curls spinning around. And there are blue waves that try to be purple, but they can't. And there's the net over everything, with gold points that go on and off. And —"

His hand clenched so sharply on her shoulder that she broke off with a gasp. His eyes were wide and he was biting his lip. "Oh, Ada. Oh, no. My baby. Listen. Listen to me. You can't say that. You have to say, 'The sky is blue.'"

"Why?"

"Because it looks blue to other people. And you can never, ever talk about seeing a glow where something is warm, either. In fact — oh, how are you supposed to know what we can see? — maybe it's best if you never talk about how things look to you at all. Not even to your mother. Do you understand me?"

"But why not?" His urgency was getting to her, making her blood throb in her head. Her eyes felt hot and slippery.

"Because . . ." He hesitated. This was something he badly wanted not to say, she could tell. "Because, Ada, people might think you're a kime."

A kime. A monster, a horror: children born with insect eyes or tentacle fingers or twitchy, hairy flippers. Kimes were rejected by their disgusted parents as soon as they were born and sent Somewhere. Ada wasn't very clear on where, but she pictured a place halfway between a prison and a zoo. Kimes were dangerous; whatever made them into monsters might be catching. She knew, vaguely, that her father went to the Somewhere occasionally to study them.

"I'm not a kime!" How could she be, when she looked exactly like other people? She didn't have antennae! Tears were brimming in her eyes. She blinked them away, but the rainbow fringe still radiated, as it always did, from her father's golden skin, and ruby flames surged from his heart. Even through his plaid shirt they were clear to her, racing out and retreating at a quickening beat.

"Of course not, sweetheart. You're my beautiful, perfect girl. No one could ask for a lovelier daughter. But people might make a mistake. They might *think* you were a kime, if they heard you say . . . the things you said to me. And that wouldn't be safe. Not safe at all. Do you understand? You can't talk like that. Not even — *especially* not — to your mother." He was squeezing her and stroking her hair to calm her down. "Tell me you understand."

"But . . ." The thought of never being able to mention anything she saw was closing down on her like a lid. It seemed impossible. She had a sense that there were obscure rules she was expected to follow and she couldn't guess what they were. "Never say *anything* I see?"

He chewed his lip. "Yes. I suppose that would be too hard." He thought a minute. "Then keep it general, keep it bland. Ada, we have to practice."

She keened and tried to pull away from him, but he held her tight. Fury spiked through her; everything he was saying seemed so horribly unfair. "No!"

"Please, sweetheart. Just for a minute. Please. For me. Say, 'The sky is blue.'"

For a long moment she fumed in silence, but he wouldn't stop gazing at her with wide, worried eyes. Ada dropped her head and muttered, "The sky is blue."

He pointed to the flowers bursting under the window, to the climbing roses shaking on the trellis. "'I like flowers. They'—yes, yes, that's safe—'they have a lot of pretty colors.'"

"They have a lot of pretty colors."

He beamed. "That's very good, that's safe. You see? You don't even have to lie. Just keep it—okay, now say, 'Purple is my favorite color.'"

"Purple is my favorite color."

"Beautiful! Now, Ada, most people, they can't see a thing if something else is in front of it. The way the newspaper was in front of my hand. Do you understand? Can we practice that next?"

Ada gave a loud, protesting whine.

"Practice one more thing, and I'll take you to feed the ducks. And we can have cupcakes by the river."

She loved ducks. She loved to watch the light spinning off their heads until it turned into a waterfall of more-than-green, falling straight into her eyes. There was a quick stitch of pain inside her at the thought that maybe he couldn't see ducks that way.

"Okay."

He got up and swept the dropped newspaper off the floor, then sat and draped it in front of his hand again. "Now. Tell me what you see. How many fingers am I holding up?"

Four, of course. Four fat sticks of red light with a softer brilliance around their edges.

But suddenly the truth was the wrong answer. She wavered. "I can't tell?"

"That's right! That's right! That's safe. You can't tell!"

"Because I can only see the paper? Because it's in front?"

"Oh, that's my smart, smart, wonderful girl!" He jumped up, scooped her into his arms, and spun her, and his enthusiasm melted her resentment. She nestled her face against his shoulder. "Oh, you'll be safe! We'll be just fine. You can only see the paper!" It seemed to be the cleverest thing she'd ever said. "I suppose that's enough for today. To the ducks, my duck! We're off to the ducks!"

She'd thought he was so happy, but now tears overflowed and spilled down his cheeks.

I can't see your hand behind the paper. I can't see your heart inside your chest. It felt sad to her, too. The sky was blue, he said, and that was a *tiny* part of the truth. It was such a tiny part that it made her ache.

"What can I say about ducks?"

"About ducks?" He used the back of his hand to dash the tears away. "You can say, 'I love ducks. They have pretty feathers.'"

"They have pretty feathers," Ada repeated dutifully. She wanted him to feel better.

CHAPTER ONE

I KNOW HOW to keep a secret. I know how to lie better than anybody. My dad has drilled me about a million times on what to say, so I've had plenty of practice.

It's June, almost the end of the school year. Our room has air conditioning, but the summer heat blazes in scarlet waves on the windows. Prismatic snakes of light pulse in the red. But if we were writing poems about summer, I would say, *The sun is bright. It looks pretty on the grass,* and then shut up.

The problem is that my body could still tell on me, any time. There are two nurses from the local government at the front of the room, and our teacher, Ms. Holleman, is twitching, she's so angry. One of the nurses looks nice, a nerdy guy with big teeth and floppy light brown hair that keeps spilling over his glasses, but the woman nurse has a nasty sharpness in her voice.

"It's a routine check, Ms. Holleman. Ears, eyes, throats. Don't panic." *Eyes.* My heart starts drumming so fiercely I wonder if everyone can hear. I might have to slip into a bath-room and hope against hope that no one says anything. My parents take me to see doctors a lot — they're kind of para-noid about my health — but eye checks are absolutely off lim-its. The nurse smiles in a tight pucker. "No need to go hiding any of the children in broom closets."

"Well, if it's routine — we have three students whose par-ents have opted out of routine medical checks. I trust they're exempt?"

For a second the woman nurse's eyes flash and her lips give a little squirm, like she thinks this is exciting news. "Of *course* they are. Which students are you referring to?"

I pretend to read. I prop my hands on the desk to stop them from trembling and hold my book in a tight pinch.

"Well." Ms. Holleman is poking through some papers; I watch her from the corner of my eye. "Well, we have Aidan Matthews, Josiah Simms, and Ada Lahey. Your father has some kind of religious objection — isn't that right, Ada?"

I barely glance up from my book, nod. My ancestry is such a crazy mix of Greek and French and Eritrean and Eng-lish and Persian that no one can begin to guess where my par-ents are from, or what we would believe, so people will accept anything we say. It's a perfect lie.

"They can wait on the benches outside the gymnasium while the others are checked, then." The nurse has a tense smirk on her face that stops me from feeling completely re-lieved.

"Can't they wait in here? It's so hot out!"

"No. We'll need you to come with us, Ms. Holleman. The students who have opted out can't be left unsupervised."

Ms. Holleman doesn't look thrilled about this, but there's not a lot she can say without seeming like she's trying to get away with something. I start to wonder if she suspects about me. I can't imagine how she would. I'm very careful.

We all get in line and file out, first down the hallway and then out into the blazing heat. It's almost a hundred degrees today. The woman nurse waves toward a bench in the sun for Aidan, Josiah, and me, and she manages to make it look like an obscene gesture. No one will be supervising us here either. All that's in front of us is a bright swoop of lawn surrounded by the U-shaped school. The nearest trees are all the way across the street, off school grounds, and we'd get in big trouble if anyone caught us over there.

So we sit, and read, and sweat. Sweat trickles down my ribs and pools in the small of my back. The white pages of my book glare into my face.

I read twenty pages, then forty, then seventy. Whatever they're doing, it's taking *forever.* No one comes for us. Aidan and Josiah try running around for a while, then give up and wilt on the bench. It's so hot that I'm starting to feel dizzy. My dad says it never used to get this bad so near the ocean; he says it's the climate changing so quickly that evolution can't keep up, and people can't, either. Sea levels are rising fast, ready to engulf Long Island. I imagine all the houses across the street under water, with fish swimming out of their windows and coral fanning off the mailboxes.

The nerdy male nurse walks toward us and then stands dithering in his white lab coat. Hair falls in his face, and he juts out his lower lip and tries to blow it out of the way. It flutters and flops back down. Oh, he does that because his hands are full: a clipboard in one and three Popsicles in the other. My mouth waters.

"You must have thought everybody forgot about you. Right?" He gives an awkward laugh. "No, no, it's just taking longer than we expected. Here. I brought you Popsicles. It's such a hot day!"

We're already reaching for them. "I call the orange one!" Josiah yells. I get cherry. Already dripping, the cellophane droopy with sticky red syrup. So sweet and cold that when I start slurping, I feel better right away. Bright dots splat onto my book.

The nurse doesn't go away. He sets his clipboard on the grass and stands there looking gawky, smiling at us through his limp hair and saying pointless things. "It's a nice school. I went to school near here, just over in Riverhead. But I bet you're looking forward to summer vacation, right?"

"Sure," I say. It was nice of him to bring us Popsicles, so we should be polite. The boys grunt and nod. Cherry ice flakes off in my mouth. It's melting so quickly that I can barely swallow fast enough.

"Summer! Me and my friends, we never left the beach. Oh, but now I'm a grownup, I just have to keep working, like it or not. Too bad for me, right?"

Josiah crunches his way down the stick and gulps, orange

dribbles sliding down his chin. He glances around for the garbage, but the nurse reaches for his stick.

"Here, now. I'll take that." Then he just holds the stick
between his pinky and ring finger. He's starting to give me the
creeps. "Your name is Josiah, right? Josiah Simms?"

"Yeah."

"And how about you two? Almost done there?" His voice
keeps getting friendlier, doggier. "I'll take those sticks now.
Thanks a bunch."

Why should he thank us? We hand our sticks over, and he
fans them between the other fingers of his left hand. Like he's
making sure to keep them separate.

A sick feeling starts gathering in my stomach, even before
he reaches with his free hand and pulls a glass vial out of his
pocket. It has a label reading *Josiah Simms*. He pops Josiah's stick
into it and shoves on a plastic cap, then slides it back into his
pocket.

And all at once I get it. They can use spit to test your DNA.
They can put it through a machine and see every gene in your
body, read you like a book. Which would be fine, except that
my DNA holds the biggest secret of my life. My heart lurches.

"Excuse me. Can I please have my stick back?" Oh, he's already got my vial in his hand. *Ada Lahey.* I want to grab it from
him and smash it on the pavement, but then they'd figure it
out anyway.

"Nope, little lady. You sure can't." He slides my stick inside the glass tube and closes the lid. "You don't have anything
to hide, do you?"

"But my dad has opted out of routine testing. I mean for me. It's against our religion!" My voice is jumping. I can't afford to sound upset. I'll give myself away.

"Ah, well." He grins and all his sloppy, doggy friendliness is completely gone. "Maybe this isn't so routine after all."

"Um, what? Are you taking about? I mean, why would anyone want—" Aidan sputters. He and Josiah look totally confused.

"I'm glad to see you boys don't understand what this is about," the nurse says, finishing up with the last stick. "That tells me a lot right there."

"So—what *is* it about?"

The nurse makes a face halfway between a grin and a sneer. His glasses flare like two holes full of burning sun. "*Ada* knows. Ooh, she knows exactly what we're looking for—and I bet I know ex-*act*-ly what we're going to find. Why don't you ask her?"

They stare at me while he walks away.

I might as well say it. I won't be able to hide it much longer. They've got the stick, and that means I'm doomed. I want to run after him, grab his lab coat, and beg him for mercy, but I saw that sneer. There's no mercy for kids like me.

"They're looking for kimes. He tricked us into giving him our DNA, on those sticks. So they can analyze it."

"Gross! How could he think we're kimes?" Aidan flings himself off the bench and starts stalking around with his back hunched, his arms bowed out, and his face twisted horribly. "I'm a kime! I'm a kime!"

No, Aidan, you aren't. Or if you are, you don't know it.

A kime? That would be me. A kime, short for *chimera*: a word that starts out like *chimney* but that is actually pronounced kye-MEER-uh. It means a kind of monster with the parts of two different animals, or more than two. And I've known what I am for years.

★ ★ ★

I can't make myself call my dad and tell him what happened. He and my mom will find out as soon as the tests on my saliva are finished, and she'll be nauseated to learn she's been raising a monster, and he'll be devastated that he couldn't protect me from people finding out. Because he figured out the truth when I was still a little girl. He knew before I did.

It's the worst thing that can happen to a parent. That's what my mom always says. It's worse to give birth to a chimera than it is to watch your kid die in front of you. Of course she has no idea how that makes me feel, every single time. She completely missed the irony of what she was doing, working on all those anti-kime campaigns, after people started to realize the possibility of kimes like me: the ones where you can't tell just by looking at them. I think the reason my dad never discouraged her is that he didn't want her to get suspicious.

The instant I get home, I run into my room and throw myself face-down on the mattress, but somehow I can't cry. How did I fool myself into thinking I'd get away with it forever? I grind my face in the pillow, but there's no relief, and I guess I don't deserve any. I'm being punished, because lying was a terrible thing to do.

Whatever made me a kime might be contagious, possibly; no one really knows. That's why the whole South Fork of Long Island is under quarantine and no one can leave here. So far, Chimera Syndrome hasn't spread outside the area under containment. Everyone stuck behind the line is terrified out of their minds of having kids like me. My dad really should have turned me in as soon as he realized I was a monster, but he was too selfish. He loved me too much. And I told myself that what we were doing was just fine.

Every time I heard my mom, or a newscaster, or our principal say that chimeras represented a threat to the very survival of the human race, I told myself they were just being dramatic. I told myself I was human in all the ways that count. Like, why *shouldn't* I see things other people can't? What's so bad about that?

But I knew. Secretly I knew why it was wrong. Say, if a pregnant woman near me at the grocery store catches whatever it is I have, her baby might not be so lucky. Her baby might end up with something a lot worse than crazy vision, or it might even die. A lot of kimes die as soon as they're born, or before. That was the first sign that there was something wrong: hundreds of deformed babies that came months early, already dead. Even now that they know to test for us before birth, it seems like a lot still slip through.

So maybe I've killed people, not on purpose, but just because I wanted to be free and have a real life. Just from being greedy for everything normal people take for granted and putting myself first and not caring if that hurt someone else.

My mom will hate me when she finds out, and I guess she'll be right.

I try to force the tears out, but all that happens is that my breath comes out sounding like someone hacking wood. I get up and grab my violin and bow instead, because whenever I can't let myself say what I think, or whenever I can't remember who I am inside, that's my way out. You can only tell the truth with music, but music keeps your secrets at the same time.

I start off with the violin parts from this singer Andrew Bird, who my dad likes a lot. But pretty soon I let go of the melodies and just set the strings screaming. I'll make the sounds that are right for me. Right for what I truly am.

Monster, I tell myself while I play. *Ada Lahey is a disgusting monster. She deserves to be locked up. Monster. Monster.*

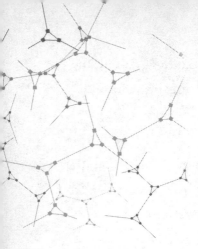

CHAPTER TWO

THREE DAYS go by, and I almost start to hope there's been some miracle that will let me keep living with my secret intact, like maybe the car carrying those nurses was in an accident and the vials got smashed and they were both killed, or the machines that read the DNA broke down and no one can fix them, or somebody in the lab doesn't believe kimes are bad after all and decided to fake my results. And then, so many kimes are still being born all over the quarantined zone that it seems obvious the tests can't be that reliable. See? I'm so good at lying that I can even lie to myself.

And it's wrong for me to hope they won't get me, anyway. It doesn't matter that I would never hurt anyone on purpose. I'm dangerous whether I want to be or not, and they have every right to take me away—to wherever kimes go. Somewhere out in Sag Harbor.

I didn't hear the bell go off, but it must have, because when I look up, everybody is leaving. I jump and start grabbing my things, but Ms. Holleman is already there with her hand on my arm—and there's this sick look on her pale, saggy face that tells me everything. Her eyes are so light they look like raindrops on a window.

"Oh, Ada. I had a bad feeling. I should have *known*, I should have—I don't know what I could have done—tried to hide you somehow, warn you. I am so very sorry."

That's why they used that trick. They were smart enough to realize some teachers would try to protect their students, kimes or not. Maybe *most* teachers wouldn't, but a few would.

"Did you know?" I ask—but really it doesn't matter anymore, so I don't wait for her to answer. "What do I have to do?"

"They've called in your parents. And there's a Mr. Collins here to discuss your results. The principal has loaned them her office for a meeting. Oh, Ada, if there's anything at all I can do—"

"You can't. But thank you for wanting to." She's about to start crying and I can't stand it, so I jump up with my books in my arms. Probably I won't need them anymore, though. "Um, goodbye."

And I bolt out of the room before she can say anything else. Dealing with my parents is going to be more than enough. The hallway is already mostly empty, and I run like a lunatic the whole way, because if I stop, I don't think I'll be able to keep moving at all. My stomach is so bunched and knotted that I'm running bent over, and I practically crash into the door to the principal's office. It's ajar, and my dad's face stares at me through the gap.

He looks like somebody just stabbed him and he's doing his best to hold in the blood.

I push the door open and then stand there.

"Ada Lahey?" a man says; he must be Mr. Collins. He has very short brown hair and a face like a wad of bubble gum, pink and slick. He's sitting across the desk in the principal's fat brown chair, and her artificial flowers reflect on his skin in orange blobs.

I can't force my voice out, so I nod.

"You can have a seat."

My legs won't move. After five seconds my dad gets partway up, reaches for me, and pulls me next to him, so one half of me is perched on the side of his chair.

"Do you know why we're here, Ada? We have some test results for you that are quite significant."

"Then there's been a mistake." That's my mom. She's right next to me, and I can see the edge of her cream-colored sleeve, the tiny ruffles around her golden-brown hand and her sapphire ring, but I can't look at her face. I can't. "Now that you *see* Ada, see her for yourself, you have to realize there's no way this test could be accurate. My Ada, she's an excellent student, a gifted musician, beautiful, *polite*—"

"No mistake, Mrs. Lahey. The results are plain. Forty-five, forty-six."

"Excuse me!" my mom shrieks, though she knows what that means. I can feel my dad flinch.

"Human DNA has forty-six chromosomes. With Ada, forty-five of those chromosomes are precisely what they should be. As human as you like. But the forty-sixth is of clearly nonhuman origin. From some sort of animal, though I couldn't guess what. That is, she meets the legal definition of a chimera."

My mom gives a muffled shriek. I haven't looked up from her sleeve, and the cream silk is dancing with a filigree of more-than-silver, more-than-lilac.

"Of course, it's entirely possible that none of that, ah, foreign DNA is actively expressed. She *looks* normal enough, I'll grant you, and for all we know, her nonhuman genetic component doesn't affect her in any way. But she could still be contagious. We simply don't know." He's simpering at her, trying to comfort her. My mom is pretty, and men get like that when she's around.

"We never gave permission for Ada to be tested." My dad's voice comes out guttural and hard.

"Of course you didn't." Mr. Collins doesn't bother cooing at my dad. "You do realize that willfully concealing a chimera is punishable by five years in prison? A law I believe your wife campaigned for."

"But no one could have ever *imagined* this!" My mom again. She grabs my hand for a second and squeezes it.

And then drops it, fast. Like she's just realized what she's touching.

Mr. Collins turns his simper back on. "Of course not. But now that we know, you of all people must understand, Mrs. Lahey. Steps must be taken."

"But." My mom gasps, and I finally glance her way. She's

so pale under her gold skin that she looks moonish, green and shining. "But—*no one could ever tell!* Mr. Collins, couldn't you make an exception?"

I can tell from his smile that he's been waiting for this. "According to the laws you worked so hard to pass? Absolutely not. You're free to take her home. But she'll have to be registered, and I think we all know what that will mean."

It will mean mobs throwing stones through our windows, screaming at us every time we leave the house. Or doing worse things than that. I picture fire washing up our walls like a tangerine sea, coming to swallow us.

My dad's arms contract so hard he crushes the air out of me. "Steps have *already* been taken! We're all living under quarantine because of the chimeras. And being trapped on Long Island has been absolutely devastating for my career; it's impossible to truly participate in the scientific community. Isn't that enough of a sacrifice without handing over our daughter as well? So we thank you for your *concern,* Mr. Collins. But we'll take our chances."

"No." It's the first thing I've said since I walked in. It's horrible, but it's also a relief. "I won't let you. I'm going—wherever it is kimes go."

My mom lets out another little yelp. I'm the first one who's gone ahead and said that word out loud.

"The Genesis Institute." Mr. Collins blurts it out, like he's been dying to say it. "Out in Sag Harbor. I hear it's, uh, really very well run."

"No. And I'm perfectly aware of the conditions at that

place, though that's hardly the point. I helped conduct studies there several years ago." My dad has been protecting me for so many years that he can't accept it's all over now. "Our daughter is staying with her family."

"Caleb, you know there's more to think about than Ada. Of course . . . we still love her just the same. But then, the stress, and . . . It wouldn't be healthy. Maybe keeping Ada isn't the right choice for our family. For now, Caleb. Just for now."

I look around at everyone to figure out what she's talking about. My dad's face is crumpled, hanging over his lap, but Mr. Collins looks as confused as I am.

"Mom?" I say. But I should have known better. She shrinks back, and on her face is the look I've dreaded for years now: squeamish and tight and terrified.

"You're worried about the baby," my dad says at last— and all at once I realize from the resigned droop of his voice that he'll do it, he'll give me up. I've always known my mom would want to send me away if the truth came out, but I thought he'd fight for me no matter what it took. I'm going, but I don't want him to *let* me go.

Then his words sink in. "What baby?"

"A little brother or sister, Ada. Expected in January. We were planning to tell you soon."

And I could infect Mom, he knows that. He's known all along. So he took the chance that I would kill their new baby or turn it into some unspeakable half-human thing?

"Well, in that case," Mr. Collins says in a that's-all-settled voice.

"Ada, sweetheart, believe me," my mom says—but she's out of her chair now, cowering as far from me as she can get, her back pressed against the ugly bamboo wallpaper. Her black hair is coiled in a bun on the top of her head; blue sparks fly from the coil as she nods. "If we knew that it wouldn't be unhealthy for the baby, then of course . . . of course . . ."

She doesn't say *of course* what, though. She'd still want to get rid of me.

"It's not a catastrophe, Mrs. Lahey," Mr. Collins croons. "No need to treat it as one. Someday we'll understand Chimera Syndrome, and once we know how to stop it from spreading, why then of course Ada can come right home. And why focus on the negative? Only one of her chromosomes is abnormal. One out of forty-six! So think instead about the forty-five chromosomes in your little girl that are just right."

My mom gives him a big, dewy-eyed smile. She's sliding toward the door.

"We can visit her, at least?" my dad says. And I know about the baby, I *know*, but my mouth tastes bitter, and my heart shrivels into something the size of an acorn, cold and hard and numb. He's changing his mind so *easily*.

"If you've worked there before, Dr. Lahey, then you must know how the locals react to private cars when they see them leaving the gates. I assume your lab took the precaution of using marked vehicles, to avoid attacks?" A half smile. "Visit at your own risk."

"She needs time to pack. To prepare."

"We've picked up two others from the school in

Riverhead, and they're waiting in the van. I can give you fifteen minutes to go collect Ada's things, if you like."

I told myself I was ready for this, but now I want to start screaming. I'm leaving everything, my friends, my periwinkle blue room where my dad painted a border of musical notation in silver near the ceiling, with diamond-shaped notes. And then . . .

"My violin!"

My dad looks dazed, but my voice gets through to him. He gets up, nodding hard. "Yes. Your violin. Of course, that's essential. You can't go without it. Yes, I'll be right back."

And then my parents are together at the door, staring at me. I almost get up to hug them goodbye, but I'm too afraid to feel my mom twisting away from my arms.

In a flash, the door is closing behind them, and I'm alone with Mr. Collins.

"You knew," he snarls. He's up, pacing uncomfortably close to me, back and forth. "I could see that in your face; you weren't surprised in the slightest when I explained what you are. You knew, and you never told anyone. Is Chimera Syndrome like rabies? Do you freaks feel a desperate need to destroy as many innocent people as possible, by making them like *you?*"

Destroy people? I just wanted to be normal. Live like a regular person and not be locked up! But if I said that, he'd just hate me more.

"You said . . . it wasn't so bad, with me. Forty-five out of forty-six. You said I'm almost human."

His upper lip hikes. "If this were a spelling test, Ada, then forty-five out of forty-six would be excellent. But you were tested to see if you're a human being, and that's strictly pass or fail." He stops right in front of my chair and bends down. It's hard to breathe, like his pink blob face is suffocating me. "Forty-five? That means you fail."

"You told my mom that she should focus on, on all the parts of me that are right! You said——"

"Good heavens. Of course I had the decency to try to make your poor *mother* feel better about this. I can barely imagine how dirtied she must feel, now that she knows what she's been coddling." He looks at me like I'm a giant spider. "They tell me your, ah, animal chromosome carries genes associated with vision. Pity we can't dissect your eyes and learn the truth."

My cheeks are burning and my throat constricts. I don't want to let him see me cry, but I don't know how much longer I can hold in my tears.

He turns away, walks to the door without glancing at me again, and slams it behind him.

I put my head on the desk and picture myself falling down into the spiraling ribbon of my own DNA. The closer I get to it, the bigger it looks, a double strand of glowing beads, until I slip through a door in the side of an atom and into a huge ballroom. Thousands of blade-sharp crystals hang like stalactites from the ceiling. The floor is crowded with kimes, hideous ones, dancing and spinning and keeping time to the music by clacking the enormous crab claws at the ends of their furry arms, twitching ratlike whiskers, snapping their long fangs.

Where I'm going, I'll be surrounded by monsters, eating and sleeping in the same rooms with them. And everything my mom and Mr. Collins said about it being temporary was a lie, I know that. My new friends will drool and sniff and paw me with cockroachy feelers, and that's how it will be for the rest of my life.

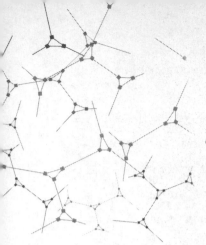

CHAPTER THREE

T HE DOOR swings open and I jump. "Dad?"

But it's not him. Mr. Collins's globular pink face lunges at me, and he yanks on my arm so viciously that I stagger to my feet.

"I expect your father's thought better of coming near you again. It's time we were going, Miss Lahey."

My dad wouldn't just abandon me without saying goodbye. "You told him we would wait!"

"And so we have. For twenty minutes. Come along now."

I try to pull away, but he's too strong. He grabs me with his thick red hands and hoists me into the air. I kick at him and scream, but it's after four o'clock, and there's no one around to hear me. Or if they do hear, they'll never help; instead they'll mash their lips together and look down and wait for it to be over. Even while I'm screaming, I know in my heart that it's pointless.

He lugs me out of the office and through the hallways with their green-white lights and green-gray lockers. Some janitor will clean out my locker and throw everything away, like the drawing my best friend, Nina, made for me, of the two of us riding on a rainbow-dotted elephant. I should have thought about that sooner, but he'll never let me get that drawing now. How is Nina going to feel when she hears about me?

My cell phone is in my locker too. We're not allowed to bring them to class.

He turns backwards to shove open the double doors to the parking lot, and I get my last look at my old life: a mirage of everything I'll miss. Nina and Harper leap in midair like ghosts made of blue glass, and I'm there too, floating and playing my violin: the song I wrote for Nina's dance in our talent show this Friday. Now no one will be there onstage with her.

Then we're outside. Red heat drips from the sky like a shining glaze.

I've stopped fighting, but Mr. Collins doesn't put me down until we reach the back of a silver van. Then he has to drop me to unlock the back. For a moment his attention is off me — and I *know* I have to let go of my home and everything here that I care about. I'm doing my best to accept it. But not before my dad has a chance to say goodbye.

I slip out from under his fat, meaty arm and take off running across the parking lot, weaving around the parked cars as fast as I can go. My sandals flap on the bubbling asphalt, and

Mr. Collins hollers and charges after me. He's strong but lumbering, and I'm small for my age, light and fast. I swerve away from him, doubling back. He can't change direction quickly enough. I hear him thud into the side of a car. He grunts in pain, and I feel so *free*.

As free as a girl with somewhere to go. With people waiting to welcome her and keep her safe and not care about details like not-so-human genes.

Then his hands crush my ribs and I lift into the air, shrieking and flailing. And that's when we both see the blue car turning at the lot's entrance.

I knew he would come. The car swings right at us, and Mr. Collins smacks me back onto the ground like he's embarrassed. My dad slaps open his door while the car jerks to a halt, and he's already shouting.

"Mr. Collins! What do you think you're doing? You will keep your hands off my daughter, do you hear me? I don't care what you think of her. She's a little girl, not some, some *creature* that you can simply manhandle. You . . ."

Then he falls silent, because he's staring at me too hard to keep going.

I run over and hug him, partly because I want to and partly because that way I don't have to look at his face.

"You brought some things for Ada to take with her, Dr. Lahey?" Mr. Collins says. Cold and snotty. It's like he can tell that my dad kept my secret. It's like he thinks my dad is despicable, almost as much of a monster as I am.

Sunlight stabs off the windshields like iridescent knives. I listen to my dad gasping for breath. When he finally talks again his voice is flat and quiet.

"Yes. Her violin. And a few other things that I know are very significant to her. Private mementos. Ada, you'll look through the duffle when you have a moment alone, all right? They're in the trunk." He sort of flinches in that direction, then stops and strokes my hair.

"I'd suggest you hurry up and get them, then. We're leaving now."

So he lets me go and trudges to the back of the car. He pulls out my violin case and a green duffle bag, but he can't meet my eyes anymore. I shouldn't be, but part of me is glad that he's ashamed to send me away—unless what he's ashamed of is *me*. "I love you very, very much. Ada, we'll—I'll try to get you out of there, I promise. As soon as I can."

"I love you too," I tell him. "I'll be okay. You don't have to worry about me."

So that's how it ends, with both of us saying things that can't be true. It reminds me of how carefully he taught me to lie. It's like we've been practicing for just this moment.

Then I walk to the silver van and climb in the back with my things, and Mr. Collins slams the door.

A stink of musty rubber hits me. There are fold-down seats along both sides of the van's interior. Two shafts of light fall from the small windows in the doors, but it's pretty dark. It's air-conditioned, so I see the two kids by their body heat before I can make out their other colors. An auburn-haired girl maybe a year older than me and a little boy who can't be much more than four. He's curled up in a ball, probably crying silently.

Of course, they look totally human, just like I do. Otherwise they would have been caught ages ago.

She looks me over. Checking for fins or something else obviously horrible. When she doesn't find anything, her eyebrows shoot up.

"You see? You're normal, too! There's nothing wrong with any of us! I swear, this is the stupidest, most ridiculous thing that's ever happened!"

The van lurches, and I hurry to get a seat before I go flying. I slump across from her and buckle myself in. "It doesn't matter what we *look* like. We could all look like Miss America. They can prove what we are anyway."

The girl pouts. "Except that we're not! It's just a lame mistake. And now they're going to lock us up with a bunch of disgusting kimes. They'll probably chew our toes off when we're sleeping, or, like, try to scoop out our *eyes* because they just have bug eyes or something."

The little boy sobs, so I kick her and glance sharply at him. She should know better. I think about going over and trying to comfort him, but the way he's clutching himself makes me think he'd rather be left alone.

"That's just paranoid. They're—even if they look strange, they're still going to be kids like us." I don't know if that's actually right, but I want the boy to hear me. The truth is that I'm not super excited about meeting a bunch of kimes, either. In the pictures I've seen, they're mostly so grotesque that it's going to be really hard to act natural around them. "This is no worse than going to camp or something."

Still lying. I'm in the habit, I guess.

We're rumbling along fast now. We must be on the freeway already.

She hasn't quit staring at me. "What are you, anyway?"

"What are you talking about?" I ask. If she's made up her mind that I'm not a kime, then obviously I must be human. What else is there?

Then I realize that's not what she means. I already thought she was pretty clueless, but now that she's asking my least favorite question, I'm sure of it. And I am utterly not in the mood.

"I mean, you're not white, right?"

"Okay," I say. With my black, thick, wavy hair, and golden-brown skin, and green-gold eyes two shades lighter than my face, I've been asked this so many times that I wish I could puke on everyone who brings it up. Just because it's an uncommon combination, why would anyone think I owe them an explanation? It's not like anybody wants to hear the whole list, anyway.

"But you don't really look black or Spanish, either."

"I'm a person," I tell her. "A girl, if you want to be picky. My name is Ada Halcyon Lahey, and I'm twelve."

"Yeah, but . . ." She doesn't know when to quit.

"And I'm a pretty serious violinist. I like reading and swimming. I want to be a scientist when I grow up."

She starts sulking. "You know that is not what I meant! Why don't you just answer the question?"

I open my mouth to say what I always say: *Because it's a dumb question. I'm a human being!*

Then I realize I can't say that ever again. I forget about talking any more and turn as far as I can toward the wall.

CHAPTER FOUR

SAG HARBOR is only an hour or so away. That poor little boy drifts off to sleep, and I pretend to sleep too, so I won't have to answer any more questions.

I can hear the auburn-haired girl shifting around impatiently, and after a while she climbs out of her seat and nudges me. "Ada! Hey, Ada, wake up! We have to plan what we're going to do!"

She probably won't believe I'm sleeping through this, and anyway making plans might even be interesting. What is there to plan about being locked up?

"What?" I ask her. When my eyes flutter open, I see clouds rolling fast in those two tiny windows. My dad tells me clouds are supposed to be white, just plain white, except at sunset, but for me they have complicated neon ruffles, violet and aqua, tying them up like shoelaces. The red juice of heat still runs across the sky.

The girl is kneeling right next to me, her curls bouncing as the van hits a bump. She looks relieved. "I never got to tell you my name. I'm Marley. I have an idea, I mean, about what we can do."

"Are you thinking about trying to escape?" If we did, where would we go?

"No! About what we can do when we're there! See, they can force us to live in the same building with kimes, right? But they can't make us talk to them! We're both normal, so I just think we should stick together. Team Normal!" She tries to fist-bump me, but I keep my hands in my lap.

"We're going to be living with them for *years*. Never talking to anyone — that sounds way too awkward."

It also sounds mean. It's not like any of us asked to have some bizarre genes go wriggling their way into our DNA. It was all the fault of the scientists at Novasphere. It happened because of some mistake the genetic engineers there made, something they accidentally released into the environment that caused a lot of kids to be born as chimeras. Mobs burned Novasphere's laboratories to the ground the day before I was born, and the scientists were dragged out and shot dead, right in their own parking lot. My mom said they saw the smoke on their way to the hospital.

"Okay, so maybe we can *talk* to them. I'm just saying, they're kimes and we're normal humans. Right? And as long as we keep reminding each other that we don't belong there, then we can get through this together. We've got to help each other stay strong!"

She's putting on this megaconfident cheerleader voice, but her eyes are wide and desperate. I start to feel sorry for her. "They have our DNA, Marley. If we were normal, we wouldn't be here."

"Some little thing in our spit? That shouldn't matter! What matters is what we *look* like. Come on, Ada. Don't let them fool you into thinking you're a weirdo! You've got to stay strong, girl!"

She seriously has no idea, and it makes me envious. I wish I could believe that just saying how normal I am would make it true. But the truth is going to hit her sometime, and it'll be terrible for her when it does. I finally give in and fist-bump her. "Sure, Marley. We'll stay strong."

The van makes a huge, swaying turn, then jars up and down as it stops, and Marley falls over sideways and squeals. It's funny until I realize what it means.

We're here.

There are a few more minutes when it's hard to tell exactly what's going on. I can't see anything through those tiny windows besides clouds, but I hear a long creaking sound that might be a gate getting rolled back. The van jumps forward, then growls along what sounds like gravel.

Then I hear the creak again, and this time I see a huge gate with massive steel bars rolling across the windows. There are hoops of razor wire along the top. Great. It shuts behind us with a clang. We swing around again, and the windows fill with a high stone wall. Then there are tree branches, spangled all over with late-afternoon gold.

Another minute goes by before Mr. Collins opens the doors. "Get out."

Marley sits there petrified, and the little boy is still half asleep, so I grab my things and clamber out first. It's cooler here; some red heat lingers in the sky, but blue scrolls of wind push through it. I keep my head up and don't glance at Mr. Collins, stomping past him through lush grass up to my knees. Doesn't anyone here mow? There are daisies so brilliantly white that they look like they're floating. A long, low building made of silver wood waits at the top of a meadowy slope, and over it all is the sound of the sea.

I don't know what I expected, but I never imagined anything like this. Under the trees is a thicket of what might be blackberry bushes in flower. I smell salt and roses on the wind.

And there's a boy standing twenty feet away, with blue leaf shadows sliding over his face. I can hear Marley coming up behind me, and she gives a little gasp when she sees him.

Because he isn't just human-looking. He's gorgeous. About our age, tall and slender, with hair even blacker than mine. The only thing that might be a little off about him is that he's incredibly pale, and maybe a touch bluish. Sun gleams all over his hair. Wasn't he covered in shadows a second ago?

He couldn't have been. The shadow of the nearest tree stops a yard away from his feet, darkness pitching on the long grass. Before I can figure it out, he pulls out a walkie-talkie and turns it on with a blurt of static.

"Ms. Stuart? Ms. Stuart, they're here!" He clicks it off and slips it back in his pocket, looking us up and down in a way that doesn't seem too friendly.

Marley must be over her surprise already, because she runs straight for him. "Oh, thank God! I was so worried that we were going to be the only normal ones here, like everyone was going to be dripping with slime or something. I guess they make mistakes a *lot,* though, because you're obviously not some freak. I mean, you look—"

At first I think it's just my crazy vision, but Marley is gaping at him with such shock that I realize she must see it too. He's changing. A cloud of reddish-purple is billowing through his skin, starting at one side of his forehead and pouring across his face like paint dripped in water. His features don't change, just his colors. The fuchsia eddies and spreads until it takes over his whole face and glows through his gray T-shirt, then streams down both arms all the way to his clenched fists. A wave of inky blue-black pours after it. His mouth is open but no sound comes out, and after a moment I realize that it's because he's too angry to talk.

Then he finds his voice and starts snarling at her. Marley jumps back, then stumbles three more paces and falls on her butt.

"Oh, so you think *normal* is something to be proud of? Because you know what you look like to me? You look like those mobs of *normals* who come slamming on our gates and shrieking about how they're going to burn us alive!"

His skin is going wild now, a million colors skidding around in zigzags like a broken TV. An older woman in a tan sack dress is hurrying our way down the hill, but the boy has his back to her, and he's still yelling when she gets close.

"You think we're disgusting animals, but you normals are the beasts, and *you* should be ashamed of what you are. You hate us for nothing, and you'd kill us for nothing, you slavering, vicious little—"

"Gabriel," the woman says. She looks sloppy and dull, with small piggy eyes and cropped mud-colored hair and that ugly, sagging dress, but her voice is calm and powerful. He shuts up at once and even fidgets a little from embarrassment. "You can tell me what you think of me to my face."

A few seconds ago, I never would have believed a boy this arrogant could look so crushed. His colors stop racing, and he turns an even light blue.

"I wasn't talking about you, Ms. Stuart."

"And what am I, Gabriel? Forty-six, forty-six. As normal as they come."

"You're different." I guess it doesn't count as blushing on him, but he's starting to get kind of pink. She puts her hands on his shoulders, and I notice that she has to look up at him. She hasn't even glanced at us.

"Am I? That's not what my chromosomes tell us. Forty-six, forty-six. Impeccably human."

Marley is up on her feet, taking advantage of their conversation to back away from them, though I don't know where she thinks she can go. The little boy from the van is sitting cross-legged off to my right with his eyes popping.

"You gave up your whole life to take care of us!"

"So I did. And all I ask in return is that you do me the courtesy of saying what you know to be true. Gabriel, what am I?"

It's funny, but I can tell the exact moment when he stops trying to get out of it. He straightens up and fires a proud gaze back at her. "You're a regular human being, Ms. Stuart. Forty-six, forty-six."

"And do I hate you?"

"No."

"Am I waiting for my chance to kill you?"

"No."

"You seem very sure about my feelings. So, look at me. Tell me what you see. How do I feel about you?"

Tell me what you see. That's exactly what my dad always said to me when we were alone, at the zoo or in a park. But when he said it, he was training me to lie.

Gabriel tips his head back. "You respect me."

Ms. Stuart's lips crimp like she's trying not to laugh. "Most of the time, yes, I do. Very much. And what else? What do you see?"

She's asking the same questions my dad did, but the difference is that she really wants the truth. The truth exactly the way *he* sees it. I don't know when I started walking closer to them, but I'm just a few feet away now.

All Gabriel's colors are gone, as if they'd vanished down a drain. He's back to icy white.

"You love me, Ms. Stuart."

"Thank you, Gabriel."

Then he can't keep the attitude down any longer. He swings his head and glares at me and Marley. "But they *think* they're normal, and they think that makes them special here, and that's way worse than being normal for real!"

Ms. Stuart nods. "It's certainly worse for them."

"I know I'm not normal," I say. "I've known for years that —that I'm a kime. My dad wanted me to keep it a secret."

Gabriel pivots and stares at me contemptuously. "You *look* normal."

"Well, so do you. Right now."

Ms. Stuart gets that squelched-laughter smile again. "And your name is?"

"Ada Lahey."

"Lahey? Interesting. There's a prominent microbiologist with that name."

I'm about to say, *Yes, that's my dad,* but Gabriel's already talking over the end of her sentence. I feel like I can't quite keep up.

"So how did you figure out what you were?" he asks, and he sounds just a little bit friendlier.

"My vision. I can see people's body heat and some other things, too."

"You've got infrared?" Now he's enthusiastic. "Cool! So does Jared. He's eight. Well, not actually vision, but sensors, anyway. Real infrared vision is super rare. I guess the two of you can talk about, um, that you can tell what chair someone was just sitting in." He laughs. Ms. Stuart is still staring at me like she's sizing me up. I don't know why, but I almost feel like I have to prove myself.

"I can even tell if someone just left a room. As long as it's not too hot a day, anyway, because then the heat all around hides it. But if it's chilly, I can see a red blur for, like, ten seconds."

I am twelve years old, and I have never been able to tell anyone that before. I couldn't even talk about it in my journal, because my dad was really intense about never putting anything in writing. There was always the risk that someone would read it.

Say it with your violin, Ada. Whatever you see, describe it in music. Never words. Music is safe.

"Well," Ms. Stuart says. She looks around at Marley, cowering back near the gate, then at the little boy, squeezed in a ball and whimpering. "I'll, uh, introduce myself to the others later. I've got to be getting back. Gabriel will help all of you settle in. All right?"

She takes off again before I have time to answer. Her hem flounces against the grass.

Gabriel breaks out in a grin. "So, what do we do about your *normal* friends? That girl will lose her mind if I go anywhere near her."

"I'll get them," I say. I can hear the gate opening again, and the van's engine starting, but I don't bother to watch it leave.

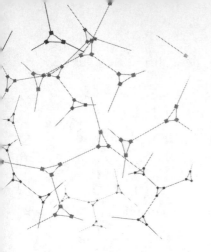

CHAPTER FIVE

I
T USED to be a hotel and convention center. The government took it over right after the first of us were born, when everyone was panicking and leaving Long Island anyway and all the hotels were suddenly worthless. So they'd have someplace to put us. I was one of the first ones born who actually survived, and I came here when I was just a month old."

Gabriel will keep explaining things in a very important voice for as long as I let him. I've only known him for fifteen minutes, and that's already obvious. We're walking up the slope toward the silvery building, sticky grass nipping at our legs and crickets popcorning up at every step. As we get higher, the rush of the sea gets louder.

My violin case is in my arms, and the little boy's backpack thumps on my shoulders. He finally calmed down enough to tell us his name, Corbin, and now he's making short dashes through the grass to look at bugs, then zipping back to us. Gabriel is carrying my duffle. Marley drags along far behind us, and it turns out that she doesn't have any luggage with her.

I didn't ask her why not, because maybe her parents were too freaked out to go get her things or maybe they just didn't care enough to bother. Either way, she probably doesn't want anybody prying.

"One thing you'll have to get used to, though: there aren't nearly enough adults here to do all the work, so everybody has to pitch in. After class we help out in the garden or cook, and the bigger kids like us look after the smaller ones. If you notice something dirty, you clean it yourself. We all get one free day per week, that's it, and one hour off before dinner. See, this is a community, and it's important for all of us to keep that in mind and not complain."

"I don't mind helping," I say. I'd like Gabriel more if he didn't lecture so much. I glance back for Marley, still stumbling along, and see the high stone wall stretching into the woods. The razor wire along its top gleams like liquid gold. "Can we get to the beach?"

"We have a *private* beach here. Just for us. So, fine, none of us can ever leave the grounds, but it's better in here anyway." Gabriel says it so proudly that it's like he thinks we're movie stars instead of prisoners.

I have to remind myself that he's been here all his life, and he can never go anywhere else, so he has to be proud of whatever he can. It's not like he can brag about his hockey team, or visiting Hawaii with his family, or anything else normal kids would talk about.

"That's so cool," I say. Because I can feel how much he needs to hear it. The cruelest thing I could do would be to start talking about how fun everything is in the world outside.

We're almost at the building. It's sleek and modern with big windows and a long, low roof with different sections angling different ways. An overgrown tangle of beach roses grows along the walls, and a cracked driveway curves past a glass door with *Reception* written in flaking gold script.

Gabriel nods. "So Ms. Stuart left it up to me to pick your roommate. She leaves me in charge a lot. I think I know who I want you with."

"You could ask me what *I* want," I say. I'm okay with making an effort to be nice to him, but he should make an effort back.

"Oh, that girl Marley? You want to barricade yourself in a room with Miss Normal?"

I'd also like him better if he weren't so touchy. "That's not what I meant. It's just, if you're choosing my roommate, it would be good if you asked my opinion." I try to think of how to put it. Something that will get through his attitude. "Out of respect."

He pulls open the glass door and makes a sarcastic little bow. So that didn't work.

We wait a few seconds for Corbin to catch up, but Marley is so far down the slope still that Gabriel wrinkles his nose and turns away. "Whatever. Come on. And you know if you act weirded out when you meet everyone, they'll never forget it. Corbin's so little they'll give him a pass, but you aren't. I'm warning you for your own good."

I'm not answering that. I take Corbin's hand and follow Gabriel up to a curved reception desk scarred all over with knifed initials. Gabriel plunks my duffle on top, so I leave the rest of our things there too. We turn a corner and enter a huge room with a stone fireplace and a lot of low suede couches and brass lamps on glass tables. It must have been a very fancy lobby once, though now all the furniture is chipped and stained. There's a huge picture window along one wall full of wind-ripped clouds and wild green ocean. A modern chandelier made of chunks of warped aqua glass hangs in the room's center.

Maybe a dozen kids are sitting around on the floor with board games or tattered books. And I know I can't act surprised, but I still jump a little as they come into focus.

The first one I really take in is a chubby boy with a face like a little pink circle surrounded by dark, shiny fur; he recoils when he sees me, as if we'd met before somewhere, though that's obviously impossible. He has hardly any neck, and I can tell that his fur keeps spreading inside his clothes. Someone cut the collar and sleeves off his shirt so it would fit. His arms look like extra-long seal flippers with human fingers fanning out at the ends.

There's a girl maybe four years old with blue skin and a plume of blue tentacles instead of hair. My mom liked to talk about kimes having tentacles. The girl looks up at me shyly, and the tentacles coil like they're embarrassed.

A boy covered in fish scales with round sequin-bright eyes on the sides of his head. Another boy with gray and white feathers and webbed bird feet sticking out of his jeans.

There are others so strange I can't even process it. They're all staring at me. "This is Ada," Gabriel announces. "She's not as bad as she looks. Ophelia, Ada is your new roomie. Say hi."

I look where he's looking. A thin girl with white-blond hair and enormous, pitch-black sunglasses is perched on a ledge next to the fireplace. Some kind of shimmery wall hanging is right behind her, but she's leaning on it like she doesn't care about messing it up. I thought Gabriel didn't want to put me with anyone normal-looking. Actually, I was sure he'd pick the most disturbingly mixed-up roommate for me that he could, someone like a collage of parts from tarantulas and worms and puppies with a human mouth gibbering in the middle. But Ophelia is actually pretty, and as far as I can tell, she could pass for human as easily as I can. I wonder if she's always been here, or if they caught her with the same trick they used on me.

I pull myself together, let go of Corbin, and walk around the edge of the room to her, checking the floor as I go so I don't step on somebody's tail. It's not her fault that Gabriel made that obnoxious show of choosing her on his own, just to prove how in charge he is here.

She gets up to meet me, and the wall hanging gets up with her. Oh.

Ophelia has *wings*.

Dragonfly wings: two pairs of translucent ovals spread out more than a yard from each side of her back. Wings lace-veined and throbbing with colors so delicate that even somebody with normal eyes couldn't possibly have names for them.

"Hi, Ada," she murmurs. I realize right away that she's not like Gabriel, just waiting for me to be uncomfortable so she can act superior and tell me how much I suck.

She's afraid I'll be repulsed by her. It's so unfair that she has to feel that way that I get a little angry, though I don't know at what.

"Hi, Ophelia." I hesitate a moment, in case it's an awkward subject, but then I decide to go ahead. "Your wings are beyond amazing. They're the most beautiful things I've ever seen in my life."

I guess it was an okay thing to say, because she smiles. "I can't fly, though. They're not big enough for me to get really airborne. I can sort of hover for a few yards, but that's it. But that's okay, because of what Ms. Stuart says."

Gabriel followed me over here. He's listening, probably dying for a chance to judge me.

I decide to ignore him. "What does Ms. Stuart say?"

"That we could change the world, and that's why everyone hates us. That we're all new jumping-off points for evolution. So, see, *I* can't fly personally, but as long as my wings give me an advantage, I might have kids with bigger wings someday. And then their kids will have even bigger wings than that, until they evolve all the way into real live faeries. And that would be magnificent."

"Faeries," Gabriel sneers. "Hey, Ophelia, why don't you take off your glasses?"

She shies back like he slapped her. "Why should I?"

"You're fine with Ada seeing your wings, because you know humans will think they're pretty. You look just like some cute little faerie on a buttercup! As long as you keep your *glasses* on. But for you to even be worrying about what humans like, or what they don't like — that's what's disgusting! Not your eyes. Take off your glasses."

Ophelia twists her head to the side, and her cheeks flush. She was so happy until he had to butt in.

"Why are you telling her what to do?" I say.

Gabriel spins at me and a tide of scribbly green and magenta lines charges across his face and neck, then spills down his arms. Ooh, so he's getting angry. Again.

"Because she has to get over caring how normals feel! They hate her, they're going to hate her no matter what she does, so she should show them her eyes and just laugh in their faces while they scream! She should —"

"They're her eyes. Not yours. So she can take off her glasses when she wants to!"

Wow. Gabriel is actually strobing. Lime green and purple and white blink over him so fast they blur together. He tosses back his midnight hair. "You just got here!"

"I'm here now. And you're being a jerk to my roommate. The one you picked *for* me."

There's a long pause while we're standing close and glaring at each other. Then Ophelia decides to break the tension. "It's okay, Ada. I'm ready now. I mean, if you don't mind?"

I hate to let Gabriel be right about anything, but the truth is that my heartbeat goes a little quick and shivery as she reaches up. All that talk about people screaming made me nervous. I brace myself and try to freeze my expression in a blank, calm look. She takes hold of the earpieces and lifts the glasses off, and for a flash, it looks like she has a second pair of big, bulging, oval lenses glued to her face just behind them.

No. Those are her eyes, except that each one is made out of hundreds of tiny eyes squeezed together. They're all glittering at me at once like facets of two immense black diamonds. Blue-green light glazes their surface. I can see Gabriel at the edge of my vision, and the expectant smirk on his face.

Nice try.

"So," I say. I take a deep breath to make sure my voice will come out right. "So, Ophelia, that's something we have in common."

She tips her head, and her compound eyes flicker with a thousand broken sparks. "What is?"

"We both see the world in ways other people can't. My vision is different from regular humans' too. The man who sent me here said it was too bad that he couldn't dissect my eyes."

She grimaces. "That's horrible."

"So what are you, then?" someone asks behind me.

Seriously? I even have to deal with this here?

I turn and it's the seal boy staring at me so intensely that it's hard not to squirm. Corbin has crawled into his lap. All that fur is probably comforting. "What are you? No one here can tell."

The worst part is that I can't even say, *Human! Why do you ask?* anymore. Because they all know I'm not. And all at once I'm too tired to come up with some new smart-ass answer.

So I sigh and recite the list. "I'm mixed. Greek, French, Eritrean—that's my dad's mom, his parents met when she was studying in Paris—Persian, and some English. My mom says there's Russian, too, from the part near Mongolia."

His mouth hangs open like he's totally baffled. "Like any of *that* matters. I didn't mean that! I meant, what's your other animal? Besides human? Because with most of us it's pretty obvious, but with you there's no way to tell."

Oh. I guess that would be an important question, but I've never given it much thought. "I have no idea. I just know I see colors where other people don't."

"She *says* she has infrared." Gabriel believed me before, but now he's pretending to be skeptical.

Before I can snap back at him, everyone's head turns, and I look to see Marley at the lobby's edge with her back against the wall. Her gaze is riveted on Ophelia's glimmering globe eyes. She lets out a quick, breathy shriek and totters, and I can see Gabriel's mouth twist wickedly. If he starts making fun of Marley and I try to stand up for her, will everyone hate me? Maybe she's acting stupid, but she lost everything she's ever known today. And I did too, but the difference is that I always knew I might get found out and shipped off. Marley didn't.

Then the seal boy lifts Corbin out of his lap, gets up, and weaves around the sofas to her. "Hi. I'm Rowan. I'd probably be scared too if I was you, but you don't have to be, okay? We're not going to hurt you. Okay?"

Marley can't make a sound, but she manages to nod a little. And Rowan is instantly my favorite person in the room.

He holds out a finger-tipped flipper. "Don't feel like you have to shake my hand if you don't want to. I won't be offended. But if you do, you might find out it's not that bad."

She's breathing hard, but she does it. Her hand takes Rowan's in a quick squeeze, and she even sort of smiles.

Soft blue ripples slide through Gabriel's skin, and he rolls his eyes. "Yeah, and if the normals ever get hold of you and tear your flippers off, do you think you'll still care so much about making them feel *comfortable?*"

It's weird to think that Rowan and Gabriel could be friends, but from the grin on Rowan's face, I know they are.

"We're the future, Gabe. Why should we be mean when our victory is totally inevitable anyway?"

Victory.

It's lucky no one on the outside can hear them talking like this, or all that razor wire wouldn't be nearly enough to keep us safe.

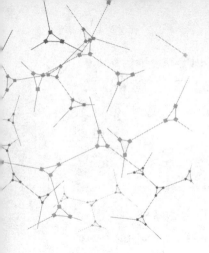

CHAPTER SIX

A BELL RINGS and Ophelia takes my arm as everyone gets up, half the kids climbing over the furniture in ways that would make my mom throw a fit if she saw it. "Dinner!" Ophelia put her glasses back on when I wasn't looking, and I realize Gabriel's right: she must be self-conscious about her eyes, even around other kimes. The sun is sinking behind the hotel, and the hallway she leads me down is pretty dimly lit, so she can't actually need those glasses to keep out the glare or anything.

We end up in another big room with round wooden tables. I guess most of the kids spent their free hour somewhere besides the lobby, maybe down on the beach, because there are about a hundred of us milling around in here. Feathers and spines and green-speckled arms stick out of Nirvana T-shirts and hole-filled pink sweaters. I look for adults, but I spot only two of them, Ms. Stuart, looking frazzled as she carries in a stack of plates, and an old Asian man in a plaid shirt with frayed cuffs. He's pushing a cart full of big bowls of what might be stew and salad, and talking enthusiastically to a small dark-skinned girl with ruffling fins on both sides of her head.

I knew that the first kimes were born just thirteen years ago, nine months after the accident, but now that I'm looking around, it's sinking in. Marley and Gabriel are probably the oldest kids here, with me, Rowan, Ophelia, and a few others close behind. It seems like there are more of us the younger we get. Those tests they do on babies before they're born must really mess up a *lot*. You could almost wonder if somebody's letting us through on purpose.

Then even with almost all the kimes dead or locked up, Chimera Syndrome is still spreading? Isn't that what shutting us away here was supposed to stop?

I wonder how many of them are my fault. How many are Marley's or even Corbin's. We've been the ones out there infecting people.

This room has another sweeping picture window looking out on the ocean, and I stop and stare at the waves curling endlessly, the crest and pull and reach of water fracturing into a million slivers of light and rainbow foam. The stone wall ends at the bottom of the beach, but after that there's a double chain-link fence, or really two fences spaced five feet apart, that push far out into the water. Razor wire coils along their tops, shining golden orange above the gold and silver water. I can just make out the line of fence, at least a hundred yards out, that encloses our patch of ocean. Beyond the fence there's a tantalizing sparkle that fades into forever, or at least stretches all the way to Europe and Africa: places we'll never be allowed to go.

So even our "private beach" is inside a cage. I should have known.

"Ada? Aren't you going to sit with me?" Ophelia is tugging at my sleeve, so I smile at her and turn away from the water. I feel like I could lose myself in watching those waves, like if I stare long enough, I might disappear completely.

"Are there really just two grownups here? To look after all of us?" I ask.

"There are four. Ms. Stuart and Mr. Chu, who's passing out salad? And then we also have Dr. Jacoway and Ms. Riley, but they're looking after the babies tonight. They're going to be *exhausted* tomorrow."

Right. Babies. It seems crazy to have so little supervision for this many kids; that must be what my dad meant when he mentioned the conditions here. "Why don't they hire more people?"

"You think they don't try?" Gabriel says just behind my left shoulder. Why is he always interrupting? "It's not like there are any grown-up chimeras, who might, ah, care about us naturally. And the adults who do live here can't leave without people attacking them. Last time Ms. Stuart went into town, some creeps smashed every window in her car, and she had to get forty stitches because of all the flying glass. So who do you think is begging to take a job in this place?"

"Then how do they keep the kids from just, like, going totally wild?"

Gabriel grins. "They don't. We try to help them and ev-erything, but once all the littles are in bed, we do whatever we want. I've never had parents, but from what I've seen on TV, that's a really different way to live. It's like the normals are always saying. In here we're just a bunch of savage animals run amuck!" He turns and darts across the room.

So Gabriel wasn't kidding about Ms. Stuart giving up the rest of her life for the kids here. I look at her crouching down to talk to a small boy with arms covered in hard greenish ar-mor like a crab's. She's holding him softly while he talks to her, wide-eyed and serious, caressing her with a knobby hand. She's almost as much of a captive as we are, then, except that she sacrificed her freedom by choice.

At least it looks like Corbin's settling in. I see him laugh-ing with a group of other kids, and it seems like he's already accepted how strange they are. A feathery girl is stroking his skin, like he's the curiosity, and here I guess we are.

There's a soft flurry of movement overhead, and I jerk my head back to look. Something blue, like a puff of flowing silk. Then it's gone.

"Ada?" Ophelia is towing me toward a table, so I sit down next to her. She turns her chair sideways to leave room for her wings. They're folded down her back, and the tips brush the floor. "What is it?"

"I thought I saw something." Something I've definitely never seen before. What *was* that?

"You think you've got special vision," Rowan says cheer-fully. He's carrying plates and salad to our table, but then he sits across from us instead of just leaving everything and going somewhere else. That means Gabriel will join us, too, and then no one will get a word in edgewise. "Wait till you see what Gabe can do!"

Sure enough, he's coming back with our bowl of stew balanced on both wrists, forks bristling out of one hand and a pitcher dangling from the other. He's close enough now to hear us.

"You mean his eyes are different somehow?"

"It's not his *eyes*." Gabriel and Rowan smile slyly at each other, like there's some big joke I'm not getting. Gabe pulls up a chair as Ophelia helps set everything on the table. "Your eyes just see in black and white, right, Gabe?"

"Yeah, black and white. Terribly boring." He's grinning for some reason as he curls one hand on Ophelia's arm. She's wearing a sweatshirt with most of the back chopped out; it's lilac with a pattern of pink and red hearts. I'd be annoyed if I were her, but she's smiling too; whatever the joke is, she's in on it. "We should trade demonstrations, right? We'll test Ada's infrared, and she can test me."

"You want me to test you for black-and-white vision?" I say. "Um. That sounds fascinating." I keep glancing up at the ceiling, hoping to spot that gauzy blue something again. Maybe I just imagined it. It's been such an insane day, and maybe it's gotten to me more than I thought.

Gabriel hasn't moved. He must still be holding Ophelia's sleeve. But all at once, I realize his hand has vanished. It's like somebody sneaked in and sliced it off his bluish-white wrist while we were talking, but there's no blood I can see and no one is screaming. I'm so startled that I jerk back in my chair, and all of them crack up laughing.

Oh. It's so funny to them because his hand is still right there. It's lilac and covered with a pattern of red and pink hearts. It even has the exact same wrinkles her sleeve does. His skin has actually bunched up to mimic the folds underneath.

He's giving me a demonstration already. I hate to be impressed by him, but I am, a little. He moves his hand to the side of the aqua and yellow striped salad bowl, and two seconds later identical stripes flow through his skin.

"How do you *do* that?"

He stifles his laugh. "Being part cuttlefish has its privileges."

"Cuttlefish?" I don't even know what that is.

"Well, or it could be some kind of squid or octopus instead. But cuttlefish is a good guess, because they have completely amazing resolution with their colors, like I do."

My mom would think his color-changing skin is a hideous deformity. I wonder how she'd react if she could hear how self-satisfied he is about it.

"But — if you can't even see the colors, then how can you copy them?"

Rowan's started serving everyone stew. It doesn't look too bad, some kind of mixture of chickpeas and vegetable chunks. "He can't see colors with his *eyes.* That doesn't mean he can't see them."

It takes me a moment, but then I get it. "You're telling me

Gabe can see *with his skin?*" This has to be the most bizarre thing I've ever heard.

"Like, your shirt?" Gabriel says. "Totally gray from here. But now?" He reaches across Ophelia's plate, pretty rudely, and touches my shoulder. "Dark purple."

"She'll never believe you if you aren't blindfolded," Rowan objects. "You could just be faking."

I'd love to hear what Ophelia's vision is like, but she might not want to talk about it. She's being awfully quiet when she isn't laughing at Gabriel showing off. Her wings stir behind her, flicking with opal light.

And I'd completely forgotten about Marley, but now I see her. She's off in a corner at an empty table, staring down at her plate and not eating. I told her I'd help her stay strong, and now I'm letting her huddle up miserably in her own little Team Normal.

Rowan watches my expression change. "We'll ask her to sit with us tomorrow, I promise. I thought tonight she needed space."

"Thanks, Rowan," I say.

"What for?"

"Not automatically hating her." *Or me.*

"Rowan is way too nice," Gabriel says. "But if he'd heard Marley going on about what freaks we are earlier, I bet even he would admit she's not worth it. Nobody's better at automatic hating than normals."

"I don't think most normal people hate us," I snap. I'm

sick of him interrupting every single conversation I have with anyone. "They're just scared!"

A *clang* shreds the air. A scream of metal on metal. It doesn't sound that close, but it's still pretty loud.

Everyone stops talking at once, looking around at one another, and some of the smaller kids are whimpering. Another violent clang rings out. Is somebody trying to smash down the gate?

"Get down here!" a voice booms. It has a staticky growl like it's coming through a huge amplifier. "Show yourselves, you cowards! Our tax dollars pay to feed you abnormal scum, so we're here to get our money's worth. Get your sick faces down this hill where we can see you!"

Ms. Stuart is up with her hands on her hips, stomping toward a pair of sliding glass doors on the far side of the dining room. She can't be going down there alone!

Gabriel raises his eyebrows at me. "Just scared? Aw, that must be so hard, to live in constant terror of vile kimes like us! Who knows what horrible things we'll do?" Then, before I know what he's up to, he grabs hold of my wrist and pulls me to my feet. "Ms. Stuart, stop! They're not here to see you. Ada and I will go talk to them."

CHAPTER SEVEN

SILENCE CRASHES down like a wave. Everyone is staring at us, and heat rises in my cheeks. I never said I'd go, but if I try to back out, I'll look like a coward in front of everyone. And of course Gabriel was counting on that.

"You and *Ada*," Ms. Stuart says sharply. "Gabriel, has it crossed your mind that Ada was taken from her family just a few hours ago and that some sensitivity might be called for? Dragging her in front of a screaming mob doesn't quite meet that standard."

Gabriel shrugs that off. "We look like their own kids, Ms. Stuart. So we can make them feel ashamed of themselves."

Something starts slamming rhythmically against the gate. All around the room kids are clutching each other in balls of massed feathers and bristling fur. A tiny girl bursts out wailing.

"You mean, you want to exploit Ada to make them feel ashamed. Did that occur to you as soon as you saw her, Gabriel?

Of course a pretty, human-looking girl could be useful strategically. But Ada is not here to be a weapon in your war." She stalks across the room to us, white-knuckled and fuming.

War. So even Ms. Stuart talks that way?

"And if they break in here? Rowan would be fine, at least until he came ashore. But what about everyone who can't just hide underwater? What would they do to Noah, or Destiny, or Ophelia?"

There's a shriek of feedback from the amplifier. "You little freaks better come to us now! If you don't, we're coming for you. You think we can't ram through this gate?"

"I'm going," I say. Hearing those words coming from my mouth fills me with cold nausea. "Not because of Gabriel. I just don't want the younger kids to be so scared."

"Ada, it's more dangerous than you realize. We don't know what weapons they're carrying, but we do know that they're enraged, and probably drunk to the point where they're not in their right minds. You have nothing to prove to us."

But even as she says it, Ms. Stuart's voice is wavering. And the truth flashes in my mind: she thinks I can help protect everyone, the way Gabriel does. It's just that she hates to see me like that, as a potential tool instead of as a kid.

Gabriel grins. His skin is bone white and his blue eyes gleam; oh, so he thinks this is *fun.* "Let's do this."

He tries to take my wrist again, but I yank it away. I'm not letting Gabriel pull me along like it's all his decision. We zigzag past everyone and slide back the glass door, and then we're both running down the hill, the grass at our feet streaked gold and blue with falling sun and long shadows.

Headlights pierce between the black bars of the gate: a heavyset pickup truck reverses, then slams forward again with a horrible metallic squeal. I can see the blurred reddish silhouette of warm bodies massed close together in the dimness under the trees. A fiery plume spews into the air above them. Those people brought a flamethrower? There's a babble of shouting voices and what looks like two men up on the truck fighting over something.

Gabriel said that *we* look like their own kids. Can he really control his skin? So far it's burst into a tumult of colors every time I've seen him get upset. If his whole plan is based on the two of us passing for normal, what will happen if he loses it in front of a bunch of violent drunks?

I can't think about that now. The truck accelerates again, and the gate groans with the impact. We have to make this stop.

We've reached the bottom of the slope, where the shadows grow denser. They spot us and a shout goes up. I don't really know, but I guess they see us only as two dark, basically human shapes running in their direction. Gabriel takes my hand, and this time I don't pull away.

We charge straight into the beaming headlights and stop twenty feet back — out of range of the flamethrower, probably, but that won't help us if someone has a gun. The whole mob stops yelling. Their faces press forward in a row of glowing ruby blobs. The last of the sun is fading behind them, so to

Gabe they probably look dark, with barely any detail on their faces.

"You wanted to see us?" Gabriel calls. "Here we are."

I glance over at him, and he's doing a great job of looking like a regular, handsome human boy. So far, anyway. In front of us the crowd is murmuring in confusion. We're nothing like they expected.

"You're not the ones we had in mind," a man booms in reply. He climbs up onto the cab's roof and stands there swaggering on spread legs. I see the speakers now, up on the back of the truck; maybe those men were wrestling over the microphone. The guy on the cab has it now. "Why don't you send down some of those bug-faced brats you're hiding?"

A few shouts follow that. A fist pounds on the bars. For a moment there, it seemed like Gabe's plan was working, but now I can feel their madness starting to seethe again.

We can make them feel ashamed—because it's harder to look at us and pretend we're not kids. My whole job is just to be a person, then, and hope that they'll *see* I'm a person.

I let go of Gabe's hand and step forward. "Hi," I say. "I'm Ada Halcyon Lahey. I'm in seventh grade. I think maybe you don't understand, but there are a lot of little kids here. You're frightening them. Could you please go home?"

And then I notice for the first time what most of them have in their hands. Rocks and a few gasoline-reeking bottles with rags stuffed in the tops. My legs go rigid, and my breath clumps like ashes in my throat.

"Little kids?" the man with the microphone sneers. His

shirt is white against the dimness, and the red heat of his blood makes it glow like a lantern. He's thirtyish, dark-haired, muscular. "Or little kimes?"

I have to answer, but I can't make a sound. I feel cold and brittle, as if I could shatter at a touch.

But then Gabriel is beside me. "Which are we?"

The man looks him up and down. "Who knows? We can't see everything you've got." A few people titter, but at least that didn't get a big laugh.

Gabriel pulls his shirt over his head and drops it on the grass. He's still as blank and pale as paper, just the ruby of his body heat shining softly as he walks past me. Straight toward the gate.

"You don't expect a twelve-year-old girl to take off her clothes for you, do you? But you can look at me, if you're so curious. So what do you see? Would you be proud of yourself if you hurt me?"

There's a brief silence, then someone mutters, "What are we doing here? Let's just go."

He's only a couple of yards away from them when I see it start: rippling amber and bronze and blue lap up his naked back like flames. His skin seems to light up in every cell—so he has some kind of bioluminescence, which makes the illusion of fire a lot more convincing. I'm behind him so I can't guess what the crowd is seeing, but I can hear them gasp as the colors beat higher, starting at his waistband and whirling up to his shoulder blades.

"My God!" a voice yells. "He's burning! He's burning from the inside!"

"Gabriel!" I call. "Come back!" I thought he was just getting too emotional to control himself, but he laughs. Loud and harsh.

He's doing this on purpose. His skin looks like fire-flooded glass now all the way to his hair. The people crushed against the gate start to shriek and stumble over one another, fighting to get away from him, and he still keeps on advancing very, very slowly. He's being incredibly brave, but there's also something appalling about it. He's enjoying their fear so much.

"You, boy! Keep back! Do you hear me? Keep back!" The man on the cab screams through his microphone so loudly that his voice rips into scraps of noise. He has a rock in his other hand.

"I'm behind a locked gate," Gabriel points out. "We're kids, and anyway you've got us outnumbered, thirty to two. So what are you afraid of?"

"I told you to stay back!"

I see a woman fall as people shove her. A boot slams into her neck, and she howls. Why won't he stop?

And then I'm running again. I grab Gabriel's shoulders, and the people who are still watching yelp in shock and alarm. It must look to them like I just sank my hands into blazing coals, though in fact his skin feels cool in the dusky air.

"Gabriel, what are you doing? You said we were just

coming here so that they would understand . . . so that they'd feel ashamed of threatening us!"

"That part is your job. I'm here to make them ashamed of what pathetic cowards they are. See, Ada? We're a team." He's smiling, but it's more like a snarl.

That's when a hand flies up and something dark comes whizzing out of the crowd. There's a *crack* that seems to be made of both sound and pain at the same time, and blackness blooms through my head.

CHAPTER EIGHT

BLUE.

Luminous and feathery and alive. It takes me a while to realize that I'm lying on my back in a bed. Why can't I see anything except that folding, beaming blue, then?

After another moment, I understand that my eyes are still closed. The blue is inside my lids. There's a bag of ice on my forehead, and water trickles down my neck. Hot pain fights with the icy numbness.

"It was my fault," someone says. Right, that's Gabriel. "It was working, just talking to them was working. It was that man Scott Held who was leading them, I think; I recognized him from the pictures of the riots at Novasphere. But the rest of them were backing down. They were going to leave. And then . . ."

"Then what, Gabriel?" That's Ms. Stuart. Her voice is tense and cold.

"Then I decided to mess with them."

"In other words, both Ada and I made a tremendous mistake in trusting your judgment. And she's been injured as a result. We're lucky she wasn't killed. What will she think of you, now that she's seen you put your most selfish impulses ahead of her safety?"

"I'll tell her I'm sorry." His voice is taking on a defiant edge, though.

"The decision to confront that mob was different for you. You grew up here, and to you we're all family. Ada put herself at risk to help people she'd just met."

"I know that."

"You knew it, of course. But you didn't respect it."

I hear her footsteps, then a door closing. The blue pulsates and then leaps upward; I could swear I feel it passing through my eyelids like a blast of static. I open my eyes, trying to follow it.

"Ada!" It's Ophelia, leaning forward in a chair beside my bed. Her sunglasses are slipping down her nose, and she shoves them back up. I'm in what looks like a fancy hotel room, except that the TV is cracked and the straw-colored curtains are shredded and there are magic marker drawings all over the walls. There's a second queen bed across the room from me, heaped with clothes and bent paperbacks. And the blue is there, prancing and translucent, like a living veil between my face and Ophelia's. Can't she see it? "I'm so, so happy you're awake! When I saw Gabe carrying you back here, I was afraid—"

He's there too, curled up in a ball at the foot of my bed

with his arms around his knees. His skin is mottled light green, and even though I don't know him very well, it doesn't look to me like he's feeling too great. "Ada?"

"Hi," I say. "Can you see it? The blue?" It's lofting upward as if an air current were bellying up beneath it. "What *is* that?"

They look at each other. "Ada, you got hurt. You should go back to sleep, okay? We'll be right here." Ophelia's trying to smile reassuringly, but her mouth has an anxious pinch.

Oh. Maybe it's just my eyes, then. Maybe that curling scarf of light isn't on the visible spectrum for most people — though Gabe and Ophelia don't exactly have normal eyesight either.

"If you can't see it, then maybe you can feel it? Gabriel, it's right over your head now! Touch it!"

He flashes Ophelia another look, then lifts his hand and waves it around. He's humoring me.

The blue arches itself, crinkling like the thinnest possible silk, and then sways just beyond the reach of his fingertips. His hand flops back down, and it follows, always half an inch away from making contact. It's playing with us.

And that means, whatever it is, it's *smart* enough to play. Did it understand what I was saying?

"I don't feel anything. Listen, Ada, someone threw a rock at your head. You'll be better soon, but right now things probably look strange to you."

I give up on making them believe me. I'm feeling sleepy, and the bed seems to be pitching from side to side.

"What happened? With those awful people?"

"They took off when they saw you fall. You bled a lot, and I think they thought they'd murdered you. It was my fault, Ada. Somehow I thought I could get away with freaking them out for fun. I thought —"

"Okay," I tell him. My eyes are drifting closed again.

"Not now, Gabe," Ophelia says. "Let her rest." She bends over to dab the ice melt off my neck with a towel, and her wings spread out, softly fluttering.

The blue dives back into the darkness of my lids, dancing and teasing me. I'm sure it knows I see it. It probably knows that I'm the only one who can.

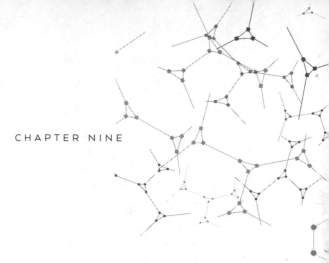

CHAPTER NINE

WHEN I wake the next day, there's a jam jar full of tumbling-over wildflowers by my bed: hot pink beach roses and black-eyed Susans. Someone brought in my violin and duffle and set them on top of the long dresser on the opposite wall. And Ophelia is just coming in with a plate of toast and boiled eggs in one hand and a glass of juice in the other. She puts the food on the nightstand and leaps into the air, and her wings beat with a flurry of opal sparks. For a long moment, she hovers five feet off the ground, and my heart skips because maybe she's about to really fly, to flip and buzz around the ceiling. But then she sinks slowly down and her bare toes curl into the carpet. She seemed so close to taking off.

Whatever the blueness was that I saw last night, it's gone.

"Ms. Stuart says you're excused from going to class and doing chores today. And I get to look after you! We can go to the beach!"

I was about to say that I'm well enough to study and work with everyone else. But I can tell from Ophelia's face that she'd be disappointed to lose her extra day off. "That sounds good. Can we go swimming?"

"I have to be careful not to let my wings get waterlogged. I have my methods. But no dunking me!" She jumps again, and this time she spins on the way down, and her speed-blurred wings look like hoops of rainbow balanced on the air. "Are you well enough to go out, though? Because if you're not, I'm really okay if you'd rather stay here."

I could teach Ophelia a thing or two about lying, that's obvious.

"I'm way better. My head just hurts a little bit now." I run a finger over the swell. It feels like someone gave me crude stitches and I'll definitely have a scar there.

"I have an extra swimsuit if you need one. We get tons of donated clothes. Oh, I'm glad you're not hurt too badly. I didn't want to stay mad at Gabriel."

She beams and starts flutter-jumping around the room, digging through piles of clothes for swimsuits and sandals. I take my hand from my forehead—the truth is that my head is still humming with pain—then sit on the side of the bed and eat. No one worries too much about crumbs here. That's one more thing about this place that would drive my mom absolutely crazy.

And then I stop chewing with my mouth full of toast and jam, thinking of my parents. It's their first morning without me, and the image of them sitting at the kitchen table, ignoring my empty chair, jabs me like a spike in my chest. I don't have my phone, so I can't tell if they even tried to call, but I bet they didn't. I bet my mom wants to forget her monster daughter as quickly as possible. She'll have a nice, pure, human replacement for me soon. Hopefully.

If they're going to forget me, then I'm going to forget them right back. I swallow my toast.

I've decided that I don't even want to know what's in that duffle. *Private mementos,* my dad said. He even told me to open it when I'm alone, like I'll get so emotional that it will be embarrassing. What did he do, fill it with framed photos of the three of us together, my old plush animals, the inlaid music box he gave me for my eighth birthday? Like I need the past rubbed in my face that way. Seeing those things will hurt me way too much, and anyway there are plenty of clothes and stuff here. I don't need to open it at all.

When Ophelia is in the bathroom, I shove the duffle deep into the back of a bottom drawer and pile random sweaters in front of it. My dad let me go too easily; the more I think about it, the more I feel like he was just putting on a show of wanting to keep me. Going through the motions. I don't know what it was, but there was a tiny hint of something phony in his voice. Maybe he didn't actually care that much. Maybe he was relieved.

Slamming the drawer makes me feel a little better.

* * *

The path to the beach runs in a thin line of beaten dirt between low brambles dotted pink by roses and white by blackberry blossoms, all of it rumbling with bees and hopping with crickets. There's the sharp green smell of sunbaked grass, the gusty salt smell of the waves crashing below us. It's all so beautiful that I can half forget the wall surrounding us and the bright blades of curling wire that keep us trapped in here — though after last night, I feel a lot better about everything the wall keeps out.

Once we reach the sand, Ophelia charges squealing down the slope and hits the water with her wings whirring into huge bows of colored light — but instead of flopping onto her belly the way a normal person would, she hangs at a slant, her lower half submerged and her torso leaning into the air. I drop our books and towels on the sand and watch her. She zips over the foam at such incredible speed that by the time my toes are in the water, she's already hitting the distant fence with a clang. She grips the chain link and laughs.

"Ada! Race me! Swim out here and race me back to shore!"

She could do twenty laps by the time I got out there. It's so absurd that I laugh too and fling myself into the water. "Yeah? You want to eat my dust?"

Once I've swum ten yards out, Ophelia launches herself again. Her legs raise a wake like a motorboat's, a long knife of water that smacks me right in the face. She runs out onto the beach with her sunglasses tipping crazily and flings them onto the sand. I can't read the expression in her black jewel eyes—they're too remote from anything I've ever known—but they're shining.

"Hey!"

She pivots, giggling. "Want a ride out? That way it'll at least be a tie. Well, *almost* a tie. Grab my feet!" Before I can say anything, she's shooting my way so fast that I barely manage to catch hold of her ankles.

Towing me slows her down a little, but not as much as I would have guessed. Froth flies from my shoulders, and water rips in icy folds around my neck. It's getting colder fast, and deeper. Sunbeams pierce the water below me and vanish into dim gray.

Ophelia's impact rattles the chain link. I let go and swim the last few feet to grab the fence beside her. My body pitches with the surge. We're both gasping for breath, and there's a dizzy lull where I just hang in place, staring into the depths where the fence's steel spits up rough corkscrews of light.

Far below us and off to the left, I can just make out a blot of darkness interrupting the regular pattern of the links. I can't tell what it is, and my breath catches thinking of all the slippery, hungry things big enough to block that much light. I can identify seals and whales, even below the surface, by the red dabs of warmth they cast. Whatever this is, it's cold.

"Ada? What is it?"

Am I just imagining things, or does Ophelia's sweet voice suddenly have a tiny jab of hardness hidden in it?

"There's something down there. For a second I was thinking shark, but it's not moving, so it *can't* be. And I guess nothing that size could get through the fence anyway. Can you see? It's over there. A big dark patch. I think at least fifty feet down. Maybe more."

She turns her head. It's impossible to tell which direction she's looking in, or maybe she's always looking in a hundred directions at once. Either way, she doesn't look over there for long.

"It's too dark down there to see anything. Maybe there's some seaweed or something."

Now I'm sure: listening to her is like biting into a plum and then cracking your teeth on the pit. She's a terrible liar. "Seaweed would move, though, right? In the current?"

"We can go back if you're nervous. But there's nothing there." She hesitates. "Ada? I know your vision is maybe different, but it would be better if you didn't talk about seeing things. You know, the way you did last night."

Anger flares in my chest. "I've spent my whole life not saying what I see, and never telling anyone the truth, and keeping secrets, so that people wouldn't guess what I am! The only good thing about coming here is that I can finally be honest, and you're telling me I have to go back to lying?"

When I get to *the only good thing*, Ophelia's lips pinch, and I know I've hurt her. I didn't mean to, but I can't face going back to *the sky is blue* and *ducks have pretty feathers*. Am I supposed to turn the whole world into one big lie?

"That's not what I mean. No one here cares how different

you are from normal. I mean, compared to most of us, you're outrageously normal. I'm just glad that you can look at my eyes and not feel scared."

I am a little scared, though. The complicated black sparkle on her huge globe eyes suddenly seems way too alien.

"The sky is blue," I snap. "The clouds are white. Flowers have a lot of pretty colors. Is that better?"

Of course she doesn't understand what I'm talking about.

"Let's go back. I'll give you another ride if you want. Even though it's not fair for you to be angry with me. The problem is, we don't really know you yet, and someone might think —so I'm just trying—"

"Trying what?" It comes out harsher than I meant.

Ophelia doesn't answer that. She frowns and hurls herself away from the fence, whizzing to the beach without me. I wait to see if she's coming back, but she walks out onto the sand and shakes a few drops from her wings, then throws herself face-down on a towel.

I swim a short way out from the fence and try to get a better look at whatever it is that Ophelia says doesn't exist. Twisty wires of light reflect off the fence everywhere except in that one area. It's far enough below the surface that even for me the murk blurs everything else. There's a big, ragged shadow, but that's all I know, and it would be impossible for me to dive down that far without scuba gear. So I might as well start the long swim back.

When I turn around, Ophelia is sitting up, watching me with eyes like a thousand jet stars.

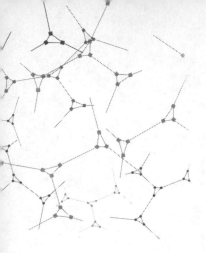

CHAPTER TEN

W E READ and ignore each other, sprawled out on the sand. I haven't seen it yet, but apparently there's a library at the Genesis Institute full of donated and salvaged books that were never meant for kids. I have a true-crime thriller about a serial killer that my parents would have smacked straight out of my hands.

Around noon Ophelia runs back to the dining room for sandwiches and apples, and we have a picnic, which might be fun if we both weren't still tense with resentment. I got a little snappy with her, but I'm not sure why she's so angry. I'm not even completely sure why *I'm* so angry. She's probably worried that everyone here will think I'm insane if I talk about things they can't see, and I should think it's nice of her to want to protect me. But I don't. My dad put on his act of protecting me for years, and I still wound up here.

The problem with faking so much is that after a while it starts to seem like nothing is real. Not even me. Maybe if I could stand on the street screaming every single thing I see and feel and think, then I would start to come into reality, like a drawing that was erased forcing itself back onto the paper. I know Ophelia doesn't understand that, but I think that's why I got so upset. She was telling me to stay erased.

It's midafternoon and I'm just thinking of going back up the hill and doing my violin practice when Rowan and Gabriel show up in swimsuits, swinging a bucket. Rowan gives me a big smile, and Gabriel looks off, like maybe he's embarrassed about last night. I'm still in a glum mood, and my mind is full of images from my book: a girl walking past a deep shadow and then noticing a flashing edge in the darkness, and as the edge shifts forward, it resolves into a knife clutched in a bone-white hand. Of course, if I'd been with her, I would have seen the killer right away, his whole body glowing red. I could have saved her so easily, with exactly the thing that's supposed to be wrong about me. The last thing I want to do now is talk to anyone, especially Gabriel.

There's a loud splash offshore, maybe just a dozen yards from us.

I turn but I don't have time to search for whatever it is, because Rowan comes over to me and softly touches the bruised swell on my forehead. He's blocking my view anyway.

"That looks pretty bad. Ada, I just wanted to tell you how great it was that you stood up for us. Someone should at least say thanks." From the way Gabriel doesn't glance around, I'm pretty sure who Rowan means by *someone*.

"You're welcome," I say, because the biggest thing my

parents taught me, after lying, was to always be polite. But since he's not actually all that welcome, I guess this counts as both.

"Are you still hallucinating?" Gabriel asks nastily, still not looking at me. It seems like he's gotten over being sorry pretty quickly. I shouldn't have expected him to care about what he did for long, but I can't help feeling disappointed.

"Yeah," Ophelia snaps before I can answer. "She absolutely is. She must have a serious concussion."

"Right," I say. "Because if *you* can't see something, it can't possibly be there. Just like, since I don't have wings, there's no way you can have them, either."

"So what has she been seeing now?" Why is Gabe asking her when I'm right here? And he has the same hardness in his voice that I heard in Ophelia's earlier. What's going on?

Ophelia shrugs. It makes her wings rustle. "Just random craziness." Her glitter eyes turn my way; I think she's staring at me intensely, though I can't be sure. "Purple sharks jumping out of the sand, or something."

I'm looking back and forth between them. Rowan's wading out into the froth, but Gabriel's standing over Ophelia in a way that's almost intimidating. His hands are on his hips, and a pattern like blue and gray worms is rippling through his bare chest.

"I was thinking of telling Ms. Stuart. What Ada said last night."

"Don't do that," Ophelia says, too fast. "Gabriel, don't!"

"Don't you think she should know?"

I didn't notice him diving, but Rowan's gone. At first I don't see him, but then I catch sight of a red blur so faint that he must be far below the surface. He's swimming with a fast, silky, swerving motion, totally unlike a regular human would.

"I think—" Ophelia bites her lip and rolls her dark stare my way again. "I think telling Ms. Stuart is a terrible idea. About those hallucinations."

I've had enough of whatever game they're playing. "Sure. Why should Gabriel tell her? He'll probably get the details all wrong, so it's better if I tell her about my hallucinations myself. Oh, except that I saw that blue thing for the first time *before* the rock hit my head. Funny, right?"

Gabriel's eyebrows shoot up, and Ophelia looks half panicked, her mouth open like she's trying to say twenty things at once.

She doesn't pick one in time, so Gabriel speaks first. "You said you can see more than infrared. Right?"

"A lot more. I just don't know what to call it. I see all kinds of stuff that we don't have words for. I think maybe light *moves* differently for me."

He's nodding. "That sounds potentially useful."

Ophelia grabs his leg. "Gabriel, no!"

I'm starting to get it, a little. I'm wondering if Gabriel never completely believed I was hallucinating, not even last night. And maybe she didn't, either.

And if that's true, then they can only think this is an issue because of what I saw.

I gaze out at the water, thinking. Rowan's vanished; there's no trace of red anywhere in the silvery waves crashing inside our penned-in sea. Maybe he's swimming so deep that the warmth of his body can't reach through the water's chill?

Or maybe that's him: that dim red smear streaking *outside* the fence.

Right near a dark patch that might be a hole, now that I think about it. *None of us can ever leave the grounds,* Gabriel said. But there's no way he doesn't know what his best friend is doing. I can imagine how Scott Held and his followers would react if they knew about this; it seems like a crazy risk to be taking.

They're both watching me. "So what are you looking at now?" Ophelia asks, fake-casually.

She shouldn't even try with me. I have her completely outclassed. "It must be a seal or a porpoise?" I say, and point to where the back of Rowan's head just split the waves so far out that to them it must be only a dark dot. "Something warm-blooded, anyway, but I don't think it's big enough to be a dolphin."

Both of them visibly relax. After last night, I can't help resenting that they don't trust me more than this.

Rowan's out there, free and wild in the ocean. He probably feels most truly himself right now, as he arcs his back and dashes under the waves.

But I've just made myself into a lie again. I've disappeared from reality, and whatever is left is as fake as a unicorn with a papier-mâché horn.

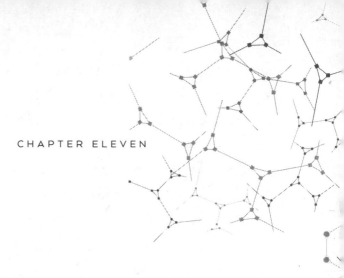

CHAPTER ELEVEN

TEN MINUTES later, Rowan is standing thigh-deep in the sea, with a long, silvery fish flopping violently in one arm the way you'd hold a baby. His other hand keeps a tight grip on its tail. "Gabe!"

Gabriel splashes out to meet him with the bucket. I'd thought maybe they were blowing off their chores, but actually they're probably doing their job right now. Rowan flings the fish into the bucket, and it thumps wildly against the orange plastic. Rowan's wet fur gleams, sleek and slippery.

"What would you say that guy weighs?" Rowan asks, and Gabriel hefts the bucket experimentally.

"Six pounds? Maybe seven. So if you can get five more this size, we'll have plenty for everyone."

"I'll try," Rowan says, and slides away again. It's amazing how smoothly he dives, like a needle vanishing in silk.

And then Gabriel glances at me, his face taut and self-conscious. That fish is obviously way too big to have squirmed through the links in the fence. "So, they swim in here when they're still tiny and then get stuck inside when they grow. Rowan doesn't catch them until they're older. We have to conserve."

I nod, blank and bland. It's depressing how easily I've gone back to pretending. "That makes sense."

Maybe I'm overdoing it a little. I get the impression that there's something suspicious in the sparkle of Ophelia's eyes.

"I'm going to head back," I tell her. I stand up, and sand cascades down my legs. My hair is clumpy from the salt. "I try to practice my violin for at least two hours every day. I hope you won't mind."

"Go ahead. But on a normal day when we have chores, you won't have that much time." She's still mad at me, but not like she was before. "Hey, Ada? I'm sorry we were fighting."

"Me too," I say. "It's something I'm really sensitive about, people telling me that what I see is weird and I shouldn't talk about it. But you didn't know that. I'm sorry I got so mad."

She glances around. Gabriel is still twenty feet from shore, waves bursting around his waist as he waits with the bucket. Her voice falls to a whisper. "You can tell me whatever you want. Just, don't tell everybody. I mean, if it isn't already too late." Her head gives a tiny jerk in Gabriel's direction. "Please?"

"Who's everybody?" I bet I already know the answer. It's strange, though, because she seems so kind. I thought all the kids here completely loved her.

Ophelia's biting her lip. She lifts a hand to hide her eyes, I think as a substitute for the way a normal person would lower their eyelids. Then she beckons me closer and I bend down.

"Anyone who might tell Ms. Stuart. But you just got here, so you won't know who that is. I'm safe, though. So stick to me."

Safe again. She has no idea how sick I am of *safe,* and anyway it never works. But I nod. I'll try to get more information from her later, when we're alone. "I'll be more careful." Ophelia gives me a thank-you smile.

I scramble over the lip where the meadow drops down to the beach and weave a little until I find the path again. The whole time I'm climbing the hill, the mystery of it drums in my head. Why is Ophelia so worried? What does she think Ms. Stuart would do if she found out what I've seen? And does that mean Ms. Stuart knows about the blue, even though she can't see it? Does everyone?

I kind of had the impression that Ophelia is in love with Gabriel. If she's ready to work against him, the situation must be pretty serious. But why?

Once I reach the top, I turn to look back at them. Gabriel's still out in the ocean, jumping to ride the bigger swells as they roll in. His wet back shines silvery white, and the orange bucket bobs beside him. Ophelia's gone back to reading, lying face-down so her wings can spread out on the breeze.

And way out past the fence I spot Rowan, a tiny reddish brushstroke on the water's silver peaks. I turn and walk three more steps, then stop again. Was there something out there in the water with him?

I look. I have no idea what it is, but right beside him a rippling shadow hangs just below the surface. It's enormous, maybe fifty feet long, snaking with an impossible complexity. There's no hint of red: that thing is as cold as death. I nearly scream out to warn him, though at this distance there's no chance he would hear me.

But the longer I look, the less it seems like that twisty shape is attacking him. They're close enough to touch. I can see Rowan's red brightening as he rises up and rests on the water's skin, then slides playfully over what might be the creature's head.

I can't make out what's happening at this distance, but I could almost swear they're friends.

* * *

Say it with your violin, Ada. Whatever you see, describe it in music. Never words. Music is safe.

What I see is that everyone here is lying to me, even after I almost got killed trying to protect them. They're playing some messed-up game I can't begin to figure out. And they're getting twitchy about the possibility that I can see things they're trying to keep secret. Like that hole in the fence. Like the way that Rowan is hanging out with some kind of sea serpent, or whatever that thing was. It definitely didn't look like anything that *should* be a real animal — more like something that escaped from an old myth. And I bet Gabe and Ophelia know all about it.

I can't describe that with music by doing vibrato exercises or even whirling my way through Mendelssohn. I grab my violin and bow, and at first my hands are so tight with anger that my tone is horribly off and screeching. Then I start to focus on the sound, and I let myself go, improvising a moaning pulse in A-minor that starts out slow and then gets faster, fiercer, higher. It's not like I'll ever get to play onstage again or enter a competition. I'm stuck here forever, so I might as well play whatever I feel like.

I play rows of jagged teeth flashing in the water. I play those teeth until they're mirror-bright and stretched to the size of skyscrapers. I play a hungry mouth that erupts from the ocean like a city, ready to devour everyone here. I disappear in notes that pound and wail, jump and bite. Because I've lost my family, and the people who were supposed to accept me for what I am have turned out to be *liars, liars, liars.*

"Ada?" Ophelia's standing in the doorway. Her eyes have the same incomprehensible shimmer as ever, but her mouth is wide and shocked. It's almost like she could hear the accusation sawed out by my bow. "Um, wow. That was intense. I'm sorry to interrupt, but Ms. Stuart wants to talk to you."

CHAPTER TWELVE

RIGHT NOW?" I ask. Now that I've stopped play-ing, I feel like I've been yanked out of a dream and everything is still a little confused. "Do you think Gabriel told her about me?"

Ophelia looks over both shoulders, then comes in and shuts the door. "I don't know! He came back up here with Rowan to bring the fish to the kitchen, and he wasn't gone for that long, but maybe he had time to say something. I asked him not to, you know I did. But sometimes it's like all Ga-briel sees are his big ideas about . . . people like us, and what he thinks is our destiny. He cares way more about that than he does about—"

She stops, chewing her lip, but I know what she was going to say anyway.

"So why don't you want Ms. Stuart to know what I saw?"

Ophelia just shakes her head. Her face is turned toward the corner, but she can probably still watch me from the glittery edge of one compound eye. "That doesn't matter," she murmurs at last. "You still have to go talk to her."

My heart is fluttering, but Ophelia might be worrying for nothing. I got here yesterday, so maybe Ms. Stuart wants to check on how I'm doing. "Where do I go?"

"I'll show you," Ophelia says, and brushes past me. I follow her out of our room and into the long hallway lined with numbered doors. I didn't pay much attention last time we went this way, but now the walk seems to take forever. I watch the green and gold leaf pattern on the rug slide by, the blotches of bright paint and flattened gum, the scribbled ballpoint flowers and lumpy dragons crawling up the walls. Ophelia's shoulders are tense, and her wings rustle nervously as she walks, and as we turn around one corner after another, she never looks at me.

We reach a short flight of stairs going down with a single unmarked door at the bottom. "That's her office. And, Ada? She's really smart. She always knows when someone isn't telling the truth. But if you can avoid saying too much in the first place, then maybe she won't guess."

Then Ophelia turns, one wing grazing my cheek like crisp cellophane, and darts back down the hall before I can say anything. But if anyone is actually on my side in this place, it's probably her.

If.

So I walk down the stairs and knock, my blood surging so fast that whispers flood my head. A touch as slight and silky as a feather skims up my back, bringing shivers with it, but when

I glance around, there's nothing there. It must just be because I'm so nervous.

"Come in."

And I do. It was only yesterday that I got called into another office, but now that seems so long ago that the memory of Mr. Collins, and of all the cruel things he said, warps in my mind. "Ms. Stuart?"

"Hello, Ada." She's sitting at a steel slab of a desk gushing with papers, but she turns her chair around to face me. Mixed in with the papers behind her are lots of bright objects that must be presents from the smaller kids: crudely painted smiley-face rocks with glued-on yarn hair, tangled pipe cleaner necklaces. Scraggly homemade mobiles bob below the ceiling. Her lids are puffed and bluish around her small muddy eyes. She obviously doesn't sleep enough, but her smile is warm. I feel a little throb of doubt: how could someone who cares so much be my enemy? "I owe you an apology for what happened last night. I never should have allowed Gabriel to involve you. He feels our situation too deeply, and it makes him reckless. I'm glad to see you're up and about. How are you now?"

"I'm okay," I say. "And I wanted to help." It's a narrow room squeezed even narrower by sagging bookcases down both sides and piles of cardboard boxes. There isn't a second chair, but she waves toward a cracked blue cooler near her desk, so I perch on its edge. Papers poke out from under the lid; I think she might be using the cooler as a file cabinet. Petri dishes lie scattered on its lid, too, all of them filled with a dim reddish grit like dried blood or maybe rust. I shuffle a few of the dishes to the side so I can sit farther back.

"I know you wanted to help. It showed a very generous spirit. Do you still?"

Is there something strange in how she's looking at me? Her shoulders are high and tense, and light from the one small window pricks off her eyes like needles.

"I mean, Gabriel said we all help here. With chores and everything."

I already know that's not what she's talking about. She shakes her head impatiently; her hair is so short and stiff it doesn't move at all. "Ada, we are here for a reason."

What? That's the kind of thing my mom says when she doesn't like the way a conversation is going and wants it to stop: *We're all on this earth for a reason*—except of course for kimes like me; we're just an ugly mistake—or *everything happens for a reason*. Then my dad will wait till she's out of the room and say, *So the laws of cause and effect tell us. What your mother neglected to mention is how many of those reasons are perfectly terrible.*

"That's what my mom says," I say.

Ms. Stuart's head hasn't stopped shaking. "I'm not speaking in platitudes. I mean, here in this precise location. It's no coincidence that our founder, Dr. Gilbert, chose this place. He was searching for something, and Dr. Jacoway convinced him it might be here. You might not recognize it in him, Ada, but Dr. Jacoway sometimes has—remarkable flights of intuition. A *sensitivity*, perhaps."

I don't know what she's talking about, but that's not the only confusing part. "Searching for what?" I ask.

"I hoped you might already have noticed unusual phenomena here. There was something you said to Gabriel . . ."

I feel like my blood is lifting up inside me. Like it's grown a hundred wings, all beating at once in my ears. That's it, she knows about the blue, and for some reason, that means trouble for me. I can barely make myself answer. "Yes?"

"That you see infrared, but some other things as well. You mentioned that when we first met you by the gate, Ada Lahey." She gives me a look like she's inspecting me somehow, then picks up a file folder bristling with bent papers. Her forehead is creased, and there's a weird tension in her eyes. She holds the folder straight up as a blind and spreads out her other hand behind it. "That's how you knew what you were, you said."

This again. I don't bother waiting for the question. "All five. You're stretching your hand out as wide as it can go. Except just now you pulled your thumb in. Now you're making the *okay* sign, with your thumb and forefinger in a circle."

She drops the folder and leans toward me. "Indeed. That checks out, then. And the other things you see, beyond the infrared? What is that like?"

Oh. My heart settles again. Maybe Gabriel didn't betray me, at least not yet. Why didn't I go along with Ophelia's story that I had been hallucinating from my head injury? She was trying to cover for me by talking to Gabe about those purple sharks, to make it seem like everything I'd said was equally pure craziness. I understand that now.

"I don't know what to compare it to. I'm not sure there are names for all of it."

"Ultraviolet?"

"Probably. I see pretty intense blues, in clouds and stuff. Where I think other people don't."

"There are a few species whose vision goes beyond that. Who can see types of polarized light invisible to every other creature on the planet. To put it simply, they see light that moves in ways the rest of us are blind to. Does that resonate at all with your experience?"

Everything inside me, thought and blood, seizes up— because that's exactly what I said to Gabriel: *I think maybe light moves differently for me.*

"I don't know if I can see that," I breathe. "How would I know if it wasn't the same for everybody?"

Right away there's something tight and skeptical in her face. What she said feels true to me, in fact: that part of what I see must be polarized light, whatever that is exactly. Like those spindly wires of light I saw striking off the fence below the ocean's surface, where Ophelia insisted she couldn't see anything. I'm almost sure this is the explanation.

"Ada, the ways in which each of us can help depends on the particular gifts we've received. Rowan catches fish for everyone, because he can swim deeper and faster, and stay underwater much longer, than almost anyone else here. Your outstanding gifts are your human appearance and your vision. If you want to help us, use them to their maximum potential. Do you understand?"

"You mean, if I see something that might be the thing you've been looking for here, I should tell you?" Everything is starting to make a little more sense. "What happens if you find it?"

"Finding it would be only the beginning. But there's a distinct possibility that it could change everything, for all of us. That's all I can tell you now, Ada."

Something blue and beaming stirs in the corners of my eyes. I stop myself from twisting around to stare at it, but I can feel it settling on my shoulders with a breathy rustling. It's holding me, and I bet it knows we're talking about it.

"But if you can't tell me what it is, how will I know when I see it?"

So far I've only worried about what Ophelia wants, and Gabriel, and Ms. Stuart. But maybe what really matters is the blue light. I mean, what does *it* want? Would it want me to tell her? It's drifting over the top of my head now, bouncing up and down in front of my eyes. A game.

Ms. Stuart hesitates. "If no one other than you sees it, and if it shows signs of intelligence, I think we can both be fairly confident of the identification."

"Intelligence?"

She nods. "That should be enough information for now. Keep an eye out."

I have a million more questions, but she stands up to

let me know it's time to go. I'm pretty short for my age, not quite five feet yet, but she's no taller than I am. She holds out a hand and I shake it, and the whole time I'm standing there, the blue is gushing over me, spinning like a tornado. If she had eyes like mine, she'd see a brown girl at the core of a glowing storm.

But she doesn't. And I notice how careful it is not to touch her. It doesn't even ruffle my hair, I bet because Ms. Stuart would notice if it did.

"What happened?" Ophelia says at dinner. But she's looking away from me while she asks, like she's already waiting to change the subject.

"It was no big deal. She just wanted me to demonstrate for her, show that my infrared really works. It was almost like she thought there might have been a mistake about me."

That's sort of true, and Ophelia's fidgeting anyway. "Cool. But I could've told her you're not any kind of normal if she'd asked!"

And for the rest of the evening, she just chatters happily about a project she and Rowan are working on, some model of their idea of the perfect animal: one that could move from air to deep sea to ground. It's like she wants to forget about everything I might have seen, and all the possible meanings my "hallucinations" could have, and maybe especially whatever Gabriel and Ms. Stuart might do about them.

CHAPTER THIRTEEN

THE NEXT few days are calmer. We go to class, which turns out to mean that everyone older than nine hangs around in an old conference room heaped with novels and history books and boxes full of gears and prisms and electrical parts, reading or writing or building whatever we want, and then every once in a while, one of the adults comes in and gives us crazy math puzzles to solve or reads us Shakespeare out loud or lectures us on the history of science. The younger kids meet in different rooms down the hall. It seems sloppy and chaotic as a way to get an education, until I realize that even the nine-year-olds are doing math harder than anything I had in school and can explain exactly how a retrovirus works. I only really know that stuff because my dad is a scientist and he taught me a lot at home.

Around three we go do whatever chores we've been assigned. I spend the first several days in the laundry room, sorting shirts and jeans with slits and holes in weird places by the names inked inside them, then folding everything and delivering the piles to the right rooms. It's boring but peaceful. Marley's working beside me, and I sometimes try to start a conversation with her, but she's sulking too hard to say much. I keep waiting for the blue to come to me again — for some reason I feel like it's usually nearby when I'm doing the laundry — but I don't see it.

I have to try to talk to it, I think. I need to ask it what I should do. Even though it probably can't talk, so how is that going to help?

After chores we get an hour to ourselves, when I can squeeze in some violin practice. Then dinner, then helping the kids who are too small to put themselves to bed squirm into their pajamas and brush their teeth. Ophelia and I are in charge of a group of eight kids, mostly three or four years old, who share one big room. I wanted Corbin, but he ended up in Rowan's group, and that's even better. Rowan has practically adopted him.

The saddest of our kids is a poor little girl named Indigo, the blue-skinned girl I saw in the lobby that first night. She's part jellyfish and has short tentacles like stinging spaghetti all over her back, and thicker ones on her head that luckily don't hurt nearly as much. She starts sobbing every time she stings me by accident, no matter how many times I tell her it's okay.

"But you've got to really, *really* watch out for that patch on her stomach," Ophelia warns me. She points to a noodley ring around Indigo's bellybutton. "Those short pink ones?

The poison in those can knock you unconscious for *hours*. The really dangerous thing is that sometimes one gets torn off by accident—they grow right back—but if it's in the bed or something, you might not see it."

Indigo curls into a ball out of shame, hiding her tummy, and whimpers until I give her kisses on both cheeks and tell her ten times how sweet and adorable she is, how she's exactly what she should be. And when I say it, I feel it—like I could smack anyone in the face, even my mom, if I heard them call Indigo a freak. Really, the amazing thing is how quickly I get used to everyone, to their spines and otter paws and the rows of tiny armored legs bristling off their rib cages. They're still cute and silly and wild like little kids everywhere.

Ms. Stuart insists that all the small kids need cuddles, so we wrap Indigo in a big towel and have snuggle time with everybody in a heap together and read the kids stories for half an hour. Lights out for them is at eight.

For us, it's whenever we want. Most nights, that means there's a party down on the beach.

There are two ancient computers in the library with the slowest internet connection imaginable. I could check my email and see if my parents or any of my human friends wrote to me. Every night I stop at the library's glass door on my way to the beach and stare at the blank gray screens for a long moment, thinking about how I'll feel if I check and my inbox is empty, or if there's a message from Nina telling me she hates me for tricking her for so long. After a while, it's like I can read the words without even seeing them: *If I'd known you were a kime, I never would have had anything to do with you!*

And then Rowan calls for me, or Ophelia flutters her wings against the window, or I think of Marley sitting at the edge of the firelight looking like she's struggling to keep her tears in. And I go: out across the meadow shading blue, with racing edges of blazing orange where the grass catches the sunset. I charge down to the sea with a sundress on over my swimsuit, leap onto the sand, watch Gabriel building the fire while his hands reproduce the flames moving just behind them and his face turns twilight blue. It's a regular game of his, to take on every color flowing by, as if he were a boy made out of glass.

I asked him once, and he told me he's practicing for the day the normals break in here: *I'll take off my clothes and walk into the woods, and no one will ever see me. Except for maybe you, Ada, but you'll keep your mouth shut.* And then I stopped talking to him, because he almost made it sound like a threat.

The only thing different tonight is that some grocery store sent us a supply of expiring food that includes slightly stale marshmallows, and they're still pretty good if you toast them. We're all perched on hunks of driftwood around a low bluish fire, leaning in with our long sticks. I'm working on my second marshmallow now, spinning it very carefully above the embers, going for that soft-as-sand tan.

Rowan's next to me, grinning at my technique. "You *would* be a marshmallow perfectionist, Ada. I get the feeling that you're all about self-control. You've got to keep that marshmallow *precisely* five inches from the coals at all times, right? And give it exactly three rotations per minute, to make sure the color is even. And——"

And my marshmallow goes up in a puff of flame. I blow it out as fast as I can and glare at it: a charred ball weeping white goo, the whole thing caught in a halo of bright red heat.

"That never would have happened if you weren't distracting me!" I'm only half kidding, but Rowan just smiles his lazy smile, pulls the burnt marshmallow off the stick, and stuffs it into his mouth.

"Ah, my sinister plan has succeeded!" Melted marshmallow is gummed in his chin fur, and I'm trying to wipe it off when Marley actually comes up to the fire with a stick in her hand. Rowan and I scoot over to make room for her. Rowan hands her a marshmallow and skewers another for himself, and she smiles at him like she means it. It's a big change from how she was acting even yesterday, but I try not to show how surprised I am. It's almost like she's made a deliberate decision to accept us.

"Are you feeling any better, Marley?" Rowan asks gently. All he's wearing is his swimsuit, and the firelight reflects in waves on his dark fur. "About being here?"

She drops her head and a flush spreads up her cheek. Her auburn curls flicker in the wind. "It still feels really unfair. That I have to be locked up like this." She barely whispers it. "But——that doesn't mean I think it's fair for you, either."

Rowan's eyes go wide, and I bet mine do, too. I never would have guessed she could feel that way.

"Almost everyone here—our parents got rid of us as soon as we were born. So it sucks knowing that, but at least we don't know what we lost, and you and Ada do." Rowan bites his lip, musing. "Or, actually? I wonder which is worse? To remember everything you've lost, or just to imagine how great it would have been to be wanted? Like, which is ultimately more unfair?"

"It's not unfair that *any* of us are locked up," I say. "If you think about it, the only unfair part was that me and Marley were free for so long. We could all be contagious!"

Something changes in Rowan's face. I can't tell quite what it is, but there's an edge to his look and to the way he's holding his mouth.

"So what if we are?"

For the first time, I wonder how far away he goes when he slips through that hole in the fence. I haven't mentioned anything to anyone about that sea monster Rowan was hanging out with, and I haven't seen it again, either—but maybe he has more reasons for sneaking off the grounds. For all I know, he swims at night to places where he's close to regular people.

"So people don't want their kids to be born dead! And they don't want them to be—"

"Like us?" Now his voice is so ragged that he almost sounds like Gabriel. "Too bad for them. There are more of us all the time, and there are going to be *way* more soon! All locking us up does is make the normals feel better, so they can pretend they're doing something to protect themselves. But in reality—"

I've never seen Rowan flare up like this. He's usually so relaxed, but now his right hand clenches in midair and his breath comes fast and excited. Then he sees Marley's stunned face and falls silent.

"Why would there be more of—more chimeras soon?" Marley whispers. She's twirling her curls so tightly around her fingers that the flesh is red and swollen.

"My whole point is just that worrying about whether we're contagious is ridiculous. Chimeras keep being born anyway, right? All over Long Island. So locking us up doesn't actually make the normals any safer." Rowan's gone back to being completely relaxed, his voice slow and patient. He's done it so quickly that a worm of unease twists in my stomach. He turns to me with a big smile. "Anyway, Ada, why should we stress about that? We're an immense improvement over, ah, old-style humans, right? What regular human can do what Gabe can do, or you can do, or I can do? I *swear*"—and now his voice shifts into a parody of a housewife on an old TV show—"sometimes I think the normals are just *jealous* of us!"

Marley laughs a little too hard at that. I don't. I'm busy thinking.

Rowan lifts up his stick with a perfectly golden marshmallow at the end. I'd completely forgotten he was toasting it, but now he swings it over and offers it to me. I have this weird feeling that it's important for me to take it right away, so I do. I can feel the molten squish under its crisp skin.

"So you're saying we *should* infect normal humans?" I ask. "To improve them? I mean, if any of us ever get the chance?"

The lights of a yacht glide by beyond our enclosure. A babble of laughter and clinking glasses floats over the waves to us. I can see the way some of the kids are watching it with a mixture of wistfulness and resentment. There's so much adventure out there, and they can't have any of it.

"How would any of us ever get the chance?" Rowan asks. "Who's ever going to get over all that razor wire?" Marley is still laughing behind me, but I'm looking into Rowan's dark brown eyes, and he's looking back into mine, and something passes between us without being said.

Even I can't lie with my eyes.

CHAPTER FOURTEEN

I'M WANDERING through what I know is a dream, something about a castle full of endless spiral staircases carved from glass. A lizard draped over the nearest railing flicks its tail across my face, and I fling up an arm to brush it away. As I turn to look at it, I see that thousands of unknown animals are embedded in the stairs far above me, animals that I know are meant to go on living, surviving, no matter what happens to our world. Dimly, I think of all the problems you hear about on TV, like the rising oceans and spreading deserts and the new, bigger, more violent hurricanes, or the crazy dictators threatening to launch missiles, and how my dad always says that we're entering a dangerous new era — but the creatures in the stairs would make it through everything and start the world over again.

They're beginning to stir, and glass rains down on me, not sharp, but as soft as sand, and the lizard slithers from his perch to kiss my cheek with human lips. It's such a sweet kiss that I'm not scared at all. It reminds me of the way my grand-mother kissed me when I was still tiny.

There's another stirring in the air, and this time I'm half awake. Sometimes Ophelia wakes me up in the mornings by teasing me with little wing strokes. "Stop it!"

My eyes open enough to see that it's still pitch-dark. I push myself up on my elbow and see the red blur of Ophelia's warmth glowing through her sheet on the bed across from mine. Feathers of moonlight glint on her outspread wings. It wasn't her.

The moon glow in our room turns faintly blue. It throws my shadow forward onto the bed's upholstered headboard, so it must be behind me.

I spin around and see what looks like a human hand made of eddying blue light pulling away. Straight through our closed door. The room falls back into moon-glazed blackness.

The hand slides through the door again, palm down and fingers spread. Glow spasms on our walls, and I worry about it waking up Ophelia before I remember that to her it's completely invisible. Then the palm turns upright, slightly curved: the way you reach out when you're waiting for someone to take your hand. My heart swells with something between fear and exhilaration.

I don't believe in ghosts, but honestly I think a ghost would be less crazy than whatever it is I'm seeing.

I shouldn't trust it, but it's come to our room just for me.

I have no idea what it wants from me. For all I know, it's completely evil. But I've been waiting for my chance to try to communicate, and I guess it has too. And then my dream is still lingering in the back of my mind, and my fear gets mixed with the sweetness I felt then. The hope.

I slide out of bed in my summer pajamas, soft cotton shorts and a matching tank top, and fumble with my toes for my flip-flops. I'm not about to take my eyes off the blue for one instant.

It must know that I'm coming, because it gives a little flourish and glides back through the door. I go after it as softly as I can, turning our doorknob very slowly to mute the click of the latch. Then I'm in the long hallway and the blue is tumbling gleefully through the darkness. It doesn't bother making itself into anything human-shaped anymore; instead it rolls like a tussle of living silk.

I follow it around bends, up into the lobby, and then out the front door. The grass shines with a pale burn in the moonlight, but the roses look nearly black. Everything wavers together in a warm wind.

It's taking me somewhere, and I hesitate, but then the thought of the walls on all sides reassures me. We're basically in prison here, so how far can I really go? The woods aren't deep enough to get lost in; you can only walk two hundred yards or so between the trees before you hit mortar and stone.

It doesn't bother with paths. When I veer to avoid getting scratched up by the brambles, it pauses and waits for me. "So, hey? You can't speak English, can you? Because we really need to talk. Or can you maybe communicate psychically or something?"

It just ripples in response, a living kite that doesn't seem to feel the wind. I can see its reflection like a million blue sparks caught on the clustered grass seeds.

"Ms. Stuart is looking for you. But if you wanted her to know you're here, you could find a way to let her know yourself, right? So does that mean you don't want me to tell?"

We've reached a place where the meadow sinks into a deep hollow, and I have to sit and let myself slide down the flattened stems until it's safe to stand again. The blue comes back to me, shapes a corner of itself into a hand, and deliberately runs its fingers through my hair. It's different from a person's touch, more like a bristling current blowing by, but it's stronger than you might expect.

"You're saying you could touch her, right? You just don't want to? And I guess you know that nobody else can see you, and that's why you've been coming to me?" Something occurs to me. "If you can make a hand, then you could also give yourself a head? That way we could do yes and no questions really easily, because you could nod?"

It doesn't react to that. We've reached the margin of the woods, and it dives between the trees.

I slip in after it. The rustling canopy overhead gleams red with drowsy birds and clambering raccoons, and only a few loose hairs of moonlight drift through. The ground is much clearer here, so I can walk without worrying about thorns. I watch the blue pouring straight through tree trunks, but then it seems to remember that I can't and starts swaying around them instead. For something so completely inhuman, it seems to know a lot about how people work.

Signs of intelligence, for real.

"You want to show me something?"

A spot at the blue's edge boils up, rocking and flashing until it settles into the shape of a human head with billowing hair. It glances back at me, just like somebody looking over their shoulder. I'm sorry I suggested it. For a sliver of an instant, it looks exactly like Ophelia. Then like Gabriel.

Then me. It smiles in a sassy way that doesn't seem like me at all and nods. *Ada,* it mouths, but no sound comes out.

There's no point in screaming. I don't know what it would do if I turned and ran away up the hill; would it overpower me, or infiltrate my mind somehow? A quick shudder runs down my limbs, but I remind myself that I followed it for a reason. It's important to understand what it wants. I need to stay brave and not waste my chance.

It ripples on, but my feet stay glued to the ground now. I'm not quite ready to go tagging blindly after it into the dim woods, not before it answers a few more questions. After a moment it streams back, mouthing something with my name in it again. It takes a few tries before I make it out: *Ada, darling. Come with me.*

"What are you?" I ask. "Have you always been here? I just, I want to know you better." If it's as smart about emotions as it is about other things, then I'm sure it can hear the fear kicking in my voice.

It grins — which isn't exactly reassuring — and whirls itself into a perfect, flashing sphere. There's a horrible moment where I see my features stretching themselves around the globe it's made. Then I glimpse a hint of thicker shapes; they look like continents. Is it saying it's been around as long as the Earth has? But really, it could mean almost anything. It might just be telling me that time doesn't make sense to it, that it spins by in a blur, something like that.

It bursts into fragments, and for half an instant I think it's leaving. Then it gathers again and goes back to mimicking my head, and nods in a way that seems to say, *Next question?* I'm not sure this is going so well, but I'll try.

"Why are you so important? What does Ms. Stuart want with you?" But that's probably too complicated for it to explain, even if it knows the answer.

Or not. It's smirking so viciously now that it's like watching my face and Gabriel's rolled into one. Then it changes and mimics him exactly, even its brightness shifting in a way that looks like the patterns in his skin. It mouths something again: a hollow whisper that I can't hear but that crawls up my back anyway.

Power.

Power, Ada. They want power.

"Power to do what?" I ask. It still has a head, but it isn't anyone in particular now, just a bubbling of humanish features, eyes and mouths gliding at strange angles. A blue hand holds something round and semi-flat—a petri dish, like the ones I saw in Ms. Stuart's office? Then it morphs again, first into crashing ocean waves, then into a tumble of animal fragments: antlers and snouts, a beating hawklike wing, a coil like a snail shell, but there are still human mouths swarming through it all. It's so much like my dream, but with a racing chill replacing the sweetness I felt then.

All the mouths are laughing.

Rowan must have been wrong about my self-control, because the next thing I know, I'm crashing into branches, stumbling over roots, and I don't even remember deciding to run.

CHAPTER FIFTEEN

W HEN I wake up, I'm in my bed, and after a few minutes stretching against my sheets, I realize what's weird about that: I have no memory at all of how I got here. I remember the woods, the blue brightness reflecting off the tree trunks and the undersides of leaves; I remember that laughing tangle of faces and wings, I remember panicking. Then nothing.

As I think it over, I realize that's a good thing. If I'd been awake while all that was happening, I'd definitely have some memory of scrambling up the hill and into the unlit maze of our hotel. So the whole episode must have been a very vivid dream. The blue didn't come for me last night, or try to take me somewhere, or mouth silent words that could only be meant as a warning. I've just been wondering about it so much that it sank deep in my mind and gave me a nightmare. That's the only logical explanation.

As soon as I have that all figured out, our alarm clock

goes off. Ophelia flutters sleepily and sends a glass of water on her nightstand plummeting to the floor. It bounces on the carpet instead of breaking, but her shoes and the book she left spread on top of them get soaked.

"Darn." She's up on one elbow, smiling at the mess. "When I was little, I knocked stuff over all the time. I'd start flapping without meaning to and break *everything*. And then I got the idea that that was why my parents didn't want me and I started tying my wings down with old tights. I thought somehow my parents would know how hard I was trying to be what they wanted, and they'd show up at the gate and take me home with them." She started the story bubbling with happiness, but now each word comes slower than the one before until they're grinding like teeth. "Ms. Stuart made me stop tying them, and I was so angry I wouldn't leave my room for a week. I thought she didn't want anyone to love me, ever. See? I didn't understand anything."

Ophelia has never asked me a single thing about my parents or my life before I came here, and I know why: she's too afraid of how it would make her feel. I slide out of bed and start digging around for clothes and a not-horribly-musty towel.

"What if they wanted to keep you and it was just that they were too scared of being attacked? You've seen how psycho people can get, like the mob that night. Imagine if we were living in a regular house and we didn't have a gate protecting us. Your parents could have been, not even afraid for themselves, but afraid of what would happen to you."

I was trying to comfort her, but her mouth twists bitterly.

"You're always talking about how *scared* normal people are. I think you don't want to admit that they're actually just mean. How would you even know?"

"Because I grew up with them. My mom was terrified. Not of real chimeras, because there weren't any around, not as far as she knew. But just of the whole idea. Like, that people might not be exactly human someday."

"Gabriel says we'll never be able to completely trust you as long as you keep making excuses for them. And calling them scared is *totally* an excuse."

My heart jars hearing his name. It's like part of me believes my dream last night was real and now I have to be very alert whenever anyone mentions him.

"Maybe he's just saying that to make himself feel better. About acting so stupid that he almost got me killed."

She's up now in front of the window. Morning sun streaked with the shadows of roses dapples her back and falls on her translucent wings so sharply I can count the petals.

"I don't *want* to believe him, Ada. When you look at me, I feel like you see me as — new and exciting, like we could all be miracles just the way we are. Like you really believe we're the start of something amazing. But when you talk, it's something else." She isn't looking at me. "I'm not the only one who worries about it. Even people who like you a *lot* wonder how much you're on our side."

When I went to bed last night Rowan and Ophelia were still on the beach, and maybe after I left they were talking about me. Is that who she means?

"I think I see both sides. My mom was pregnant when I left. So, Ophelia, if the baby dies because I infected my mom, how could I feel okay about that? I would be a murderer. That's all I'm saying. I understand why they're scared, because I am too."

I don't say, *You've been in here all your life, so you've never had to worry about anything like that happening.*

"Well, what if the baby is like me? Or what if she can fly for real? Would you still feel bad, if you wind up with a little sister who's an actual faerie? Normal people don't even use the sky, anyway, except for airplanes, so I don't see why it shouldn't belong to us."

It's one of those funny moments when you can see into someone else's mind. I feel like I'm watching every daydream Ophelia ever had, all filled with the flash and spin of dragonfly people: a whole kingdom of them, somersaulting over the treetops. She's waiting for that day so passionately that it sends a twitch through her wings, even if she won't be alive to see it. And I know what I should say: *Are you kidding? It would be awesome if I had a sister like you!*

But I can't do it. "I'd still feel bad, because it would be hard for her. Just like it's hard for us."

She starts to turn and stops abruptly with her wings quivering, watching me from the edge of one faceted eye. And I know it was the wrong thing to say, and she'll think it means I'm not trustworthy. Though not trustworthy for what?

I think of what the blue said in my dream. *They want power.* That might be true for Gabriel, but I'm sure that's not what

Ophelia's wishing for. I've seen her dreams like they were shining straight into me.

She wants the sky.

"Ada?" Ophelia has turned around now as she shimmies one of her chopped-up shirts past her hips and shoves both hands into the sleeves. Of course she can never pull on anything over her head. "What happened to your legs?"

I guess there is a stinging sensation in my calves. I've been doing my best to ignore it.

When I look down, both shins are scored all over with deep scratches and smudges of dried blood. Just as if I'd run in a frenzy through blackberry bushes, with no awareness at all of where I was going. I stare at my legs and then back at her, and I just can't make myself answer.

CHAPTER SIXTEEN

I

T'S A hot day and there's no money for air conditioning, so every window in our conference room is
propped open with ancient textbooks or donated boots
three sizes too big for any of the kids here. Dr. Jacoway
comes shuffling in to give us one of his dreamy lectures on
science. He's an old man, as fat and gray and sad-looking as
a storm cloud. Below his too-short pants his ankles pouch
in such thick rolls of ashy flesh that, if I didn't know better,
I seriously might think he was a kime too, maybe part wal-
rus. A few of the younger kids start giggling, just watching
him walk in.

"Origins," he murmurs, then waits, maybe for us to be
quiet or maybe until he can remember where he is. "How
many human myths — and please know I include you in that
heartbreaking category, human, yes, *Homo mutandus* every one
of you children — concern origins, whether of some aspect

of our universe or ourselves? The origins of life, thought, the sun? Now we have a new origination to consider: yours."

There's an awkward silence, but except for a few titters, no one interrupts. Everyone knows this is just how Dr. Jacoway acts. He stares into the corner, and his face looks like it's melting down a drain. It took me a few days to get over constantly worrying that he was about to start sobbing.

"So: tell me the story. How did the chimeras come into being? Make it mythic, please, my dears. Make it a grand enough narrative to be worthy of you. Give yourselves something to live up to."

He falls silent, and his eyes roll sleepily from one face to the next. Is he actually waiting for someone to raise a hand? What's the point, when everyone knows the story anyway? There's nothing all that mythic about a bunch of bored scientists at Novasphere getting sloppy and dropping a test tube or whatever happened. We all look around at one another, eyebrows raised and antennae fidgeting.

The totally amazing thing is that Marley puts up her hand. It's a shock, because as far as I can remember, she hasn't spoken once in class, just slumped in the corner with a book. And even though she kept turning the pages, you could tell she wasn't really focused on them.

Dr. Jacoway doesn't call on her, just gapes in complete bafflement. Marley looks almost too abashed to talk, but then she does anyway.

"I think we're being punished by God," she says, so softly

it's hard to hear her. "For how people have hurt the planet so much, and made so many species go extinct. So, like, now *we* have to be the animals. But it's not fair, because we're just kids! We're not the ones who even did it."

By the last sentence her voice is cracking. The whole room falls into a stunned silence, and Marley buries her face in her crossed arms. It's the second time she's said something a lot more interesting than I would have expected — but even bigger than that, Marley used the word *we*.

"I rather consider you children a great blessing, my dear," Dr. Jacoway says, with an awkward little laugh. "Please don't envision yourself accursed."

I get up to go sit beside her, to try to comfort her somehow. She sees me coming and jumps up, crimson-faced, and storms from the room. The door slams, and there's another aching silence.

"Poor child," Dr. Jacoway murmurs. "Well, let her go for now, let her go. Any other thoughts?" Silence. I think about following Marley, but it seems like she'll just get mad if I do. Maybe Dr. Jacoway is right.

"Um, probably it was a retrovirus?" Rowan says at last. "They experiment with retroviruses for genetic engineering anyway, because viruses like that copy themselves over DNA that's already there. So, say, if they engineered a really powerful virus and then it mutated and started shuffling random genes around?"

That's what a lot of people assumed. My dad explained to

me once why that couldn't be right, though. But it's a relief to think about an explanation so calm and rational after Marley's. It's like Rowan's voice cleared away all the tension, and everyone can start breathing normally again.

Dr. Jacoway nods to himself at the front of the room, his eyelids drooping like he's listening to a symphony. He never looks anyone straight in the face for more than half a second. "Insufficiently glorious, I think, Rowan. If we were seeking to explain, oh, a genetic tendency to acne, or to pattern baldness, that might be a story adequate to the case. But it's much too trivial to account for anything so astounding as yourselves. Try again."

Ophelia laughs sharply. "The sun got bored with regular humans, so it burned holes in their DNA and replaced it with coiled-up sunbeams that *pretended* to be DNA from different animals! And it was a great invention, because the chimeras were the most magical thing the world had ever seen."

She has her glasses on and I can't tell where she's looking, but the words seem aimed at me — or maybe at Marley, even though she can't hear them.

I rub my legs together, feeling the scabbed ridges of my scratches. I know now that can't have been a dream last night, no matter how much the idea that it was real scares me. I just wish I'd been brave enough to find out what the blue wanted to show me.

Dr. Jacoway sways on his feet, mulling Ophelia's version. "Pretty," he admits at last. "A pretty story. That's a beginning, certainly. But it lacks the fervor, the bite that transcends mere prettiness and attains the genuine sublime. Real myths aren't quite so self-serving, in any case."

Gabriel snorts in irritation and flops his head down on the table. His skin crawls with blue and lavender static.

"It couldn't have been a virus," I say. "That's what my dad told me. Viruses can insert genes into DNA, but not very many genes, because they're just too small to carry that much information. We have entire chromosomes copied from other species. Like, if you imagine we're books, then a virus could slip in a few *words* from other animals, but we have whole chapters! There's no way a virus could do that."

Dr. Jacoway turns to me, blinking as if I'd thrown a bucket of water over his head. "Ha. And where did you come from, inexplicable child? *Another* one, indeed, in the space of ten minutes! Have I seen you before?"

He knows all the kids he helped raise from the time they were babies, but he can't seem to remember me or Marley at all. I've been introduced to him three times already. There's a new flurry of giggling.

"I'm Ada. I got here almost a week ago."

"Your dad, you say, no less. *Homo mutandus* by analysis, then, but by neither appearance nor upbringing? A wisp of the other under cover of *sapiens*? Am I correct?"

Almost everyone is fizzling with stifled laughter now. Ophelia has one hand clamped over her mouth. I try to tell myself that it's the situation that's funny, and that they're not laughing at me.

"That sounds right?" I tell him. More or less, anyway.

"Ah. Perhaps your passage here from other spheres will allow you to bring us some sorely needed perspective. It was not a virus, you say, that sparked your existence. Your reasoning seems apt. What then?"

It was a mistake to mention my dad; it just makes everyone resent me. "There are parasitic algae that can do the same thing a retrovirus does: they invade cells and write over sections of DNA. But because algae are a lot bigger, scientists could engineer them to copy whole chromosomes from whatever animal they infected first, then when they moved on and infected people, they could write those chromosomes over big chunks of human DNA. In theory, that could have been how it happened."

It's just a theory. Since the scientists at Novasphere who worked on the project were murdered and their computers were burned, it doesn't seem like anyone is ever going to know the details.

Rowan looks impressed and gives me a quick thumbs-up, curling his fingers into his flipper. So even if we were arguing last night, he's still my friend, anyway. Gabriel doesn't look up from the table, but I notice his mouth tighten as a flare of red shoots through his cheek. What's aggravated him this time?

"Algae," Dr. Jacoway muses. "Algae. Yes, that's better. The crash of the waves, the inexorable drag of the tides, Aphrodite herself emerging from the foam. And the chimeras appeared, as we know, here on Long Island, a spit of land caught between sea and sea. Perhaps indeed we may find that all of you are a dream cast on our shores."

Gabriel lifts his head up, scowling. He's never quiet for this long. "Are you for real, Dr. Jacoway? *Aphrodite?* That has nothing to do with anything. We're not some dream. We're the new reality."

At my old school nobody ever would have gotten away with being so rude to a teacher, but Dr. Jacoway just bobs his head and flaps his arms with this slow, vague beat. The breeze from the open window stirs his gray scribble of hair. He looks pretty absurd, but no one's laughing now. All at once there's a sense in the room that whatever is happening is crushingly serious.

"A fair objection, my angel Gabriel. But. Watson and Crick, Gabriel. Their discovery of the structure of DNA."

"So they discovered it." Gabriel isn't even pretending to show respect. Dr. Jacoway has his problems, but he's much too nice to be treated this way. "We know that."

"They considered a number of structures DNA might have. There was more than one possibility, you see. But they pursued the famous double helix because of its *beauty.* Because it was a spiral staircase fit for life itself to climb, like a lady elegantly ascending to nature's present multiplicity. Their intuition proved correct. Beauty is what led them to the truth, Gabriel. May it do the same for us."

No matter how bad the blue creeped me out last night, I have to admit that it's always been beautiful: as changeable and wild as moonlight on water, but smart, playful, and so free. And leading me to the truth was probably exactly what it wanted to do. I just couldn't handle it. My legs tense with the urge to run straight back to the woods. I need to go there alone as soon as I possibly can. Search for whatever it wanted me to see.

Gabriel's fuming, the static on his skin speeding up and shifting green and orange. "I don't think the truth is beautiful. It's usually ugly as dirt. What was so beautiful about your friends getting their brains blown out?"

Dr. Jacoway's *friends?* What is Gabe saying?

"Will you think me heartless, Gabriel, if I tell you that it was? It's no use to pronounce to me how ugly it *ought* to have been. I was there. I saw it for myself. The supernovas of gore on the windshields, the hands clawing at glittering asphalt, the sun reflecting on the pool of my own blood as I neared death. I have never been the same. I know far better than you can how my mind was shattered that day, and what wonderful people were lost. But in my own grief, in my own brokenness, I still see stars."

CHAPTER SEVENTEEN

I CAN'T RUN out on class or chores without everyone
noticing. I go through the motions for the rest of the
day, scooping hot laundry from the dryers and folding tiny
shirts. This time I get a stack of Indigo's clothes, their backs
covered in brownish burns from her tentacles. Marley scowls
nearby, never making eye contact. She's folding clothes like
her hands are almost too heavy to move.

"I liked what you said in class," I try, after a while. "I
mean, I don't think it's actually like that. But it was still interesting."

She gives me a sidelong look, like I might be making fun
of her, but I guess whatever she sees in my face helps her trust
me a little.

"I wish I'd kept my mouth shut! When I was at home, I
never thought about anything like that. But here there's nothing *else* to do, and suddenly I can't stop all these horrible ideas
from coming in my head. I need to stop thinking so much."

"Why *shouldn't* you think about everything that's happened? There's a lot to figure out." I take a deep breath. At home, I know, we never would have had anything to do with each other, maybe said hi in the hallway at most. I would think she was bland and boring, and she'd probably think I was a weird know-it-all. Here, though, she must be feeling really alone—and anyway she's starting to change. Maybe into someone I could sincerely like. "It's *cool* that you're trying to understand stuff!"

"Ada?" Marley asks. Is her lip trembling? "You don't think having thoughts like that means there's something wrong with me? I almost feel like there's something happening in my brain. And then, my parents were always taking me to doctors, way more than normal, and I wonder if they knew— that I was messed up somehow."

I give her shoulders a quick half hug; I got dragged to doctors a lot too, and learning that Marley was as well nags at me, like it might mean something. But right now what matters is showing her some support.

"If there's something happening to you, I think it's probably positive. Like, it was hard for you coming here, but now it's making you stronger. That's all."

Marley manages a smile, and after that I notice she's working a little more quickly.

The whole time I'm pouring in detergent and loading the machines, I can't stop wondering about Dr. Jacoway. Did he really survive the massacre at Novasphere? Everyone seemed freaked out by what he was saying, but no one acted surprised;

they obviously knew the story already. So why did he ask us where chimeras came from, when he might be the only person alive who knows the whole truth? Or was he so devastated that he lost part of his memory? He definitely acts like he might have some kind of brain damage.

The second the clock hits five, I tell Marley I have to get to the bathroom and then I dash out, up stairs and around bends; it generally takes ten minutes or so for everyone to finish whatever they're doing and drift to the lobby or the beach. As I step out the front door, my hair swirls in a gust smelling of trampled wildflowers and pine.

I want to reach the woods before anybody sees me. I can always say that I was just going for a walk, but what if someone tries to tag along?

As long as I'm in view of the windows, I walk slowly, watching the coils of red heat tangling with the wind, which is aqua and silver and a blue like dusk, but brighter. Every sunbeam striking the grass and leaves scatters a violet fringe over the air. The metallic buzz of insects carpets the ground. I sit to glide down the same grassy hollow as last night.

Once I reach the tree shadows, I stop and glance around. Three of the smaller kids are skipping rope near the main entrance, then the hill streaks down filled with nothing but daisies. Red smolders everywhere, it's so hot out, but there's nowhere much anyone could hide in the meadow. I wander along the wood's edge for a while, trying to find the exact spot where the blue led me in among the trees. It's probably annoyed with how I acted last night, so I have to assume it won't be coming to help me out. I'm on my own.

It all looks so different in daylight that I can't be sure, but I think I recognize a branch bent like an elbow. Maybe the woods here don't go too far back, but it's just hitting me now how unlikely it is that I'll find whatever it is I'm looking for. It could be as small as an ant; it could be hidden under a root; I'll probably walk right past it and have no idea. The shadows thicken until it's like walking through green glass shading up to ruby where the rising heat gets trapped by the branches. It's cooler in here, quieter, with no sounds but a few rustlings and the swoop of bird song.

The rustling is a tiny bit too cautious, too conscious-sounding, for an animal.

I had a feeling that this was going to happen. Gabriel and maybe even Ophelia are getting too paranoid about me to let me just wander off on my own. I crouch down pretending to look at a ruffled yellow mushroom, then glance around. The heat today is pretty good camouflage, but in the shade it's not body temperature, and there's an upright shape back there that's a touch brighter than its surroundings. Whoever it is, they're trying to hide behind a spruce.

"Hi," I call. I'd assumed at first the shape was Gabriel, but now I'm wondering if it's too thick for him. "I can see you, so you might as well come out."

Rowan gives a theatrical sigh and walks around the tree. "Sorry, Ada. Now you'll really think I'm a dork."

I'm so completely disappointed in him that for a moment I just stare, and he bends down to tug at a loose branch that got caught in his shoelace.

"I didn't think you were someone who would do this. Like, *spy* on me? Rowan, come on!"

"You could give me the benefit of the doubt. That I have a good reason for it, and that I'm — as much on your side as I can be, considering what I am. I remember what you did for us, Ada. That means a lot to me." He raises one flipper-hand as if he were reaching out to touch the stitches on my forehead, though he's still too far away.

"But not to Gabriel," I say. "It doesn't matter to him at all. Not to Ophelia, either."

He walks closer, shaking his head. He doesn't really have a neck, so the movement makes his fur bulge out above his shirt.

"Ophelia's on your side, too. As much as *she* can be. So, hey, where are you heading, anyway?" He grins, but his eyes look sad.

"I'm out for a walk."

He grimaces. "You know, I'm not Gabriel. Just because he's my friend doesn't mean you have to act like I'm some kind of extension of him."

"If you're following me, you're probably reporting back to *somebody*. But I don't even know where I'm going, so that wasn't a lie."

I sound defensive. Do I really think I owe it to Rowan to tell him everything?

Rowan tips his head, considering that. "Okay, so I am. Reporting on you. But not to Gabriel, and not because I want to get you in trouble. Believe it or not, I'm trying to keep you *out* of trouble."

I turn to walk on, and Rowan stays close beside me, just as if I'd gone exploring with him on purpose. He's not really built for moving quietly through woods, and his sneakers shuffle and snap twigs way more than mine do.

"If it's not to Gabriel, then it must be to Ms. Stuart."

"Good guess. She thinks you might be hiding something important. So, if I follow you, then I can tell her that you were just sitting on a log and daydreaming or whatever. Not—doing anything she'd be upset about. See? I'm on your side."

"What does she *think* I'm doing?"

"Maybe sneaking out here to have long conversations with some invisible entity? Think of how you'd feel if you'd been looking for something for thirteen years, and you suspected that the *one* person who might have the ability to see it had decided to keep it a secret. You'd be seriously pissed. And she's smart to be suspicious of you, anyway. I haven't said anything to her, but I'm almost positive you've seen things here and just pretended to have no idea. Right? Are you going to come out and say it, or should I?"

I guess I'm not surprised that he knows so much. He stops with his hand on my shoulder, and gently tugs me around to look at him. His pink face gleams with sweat—it must be terrible having fur in this weather—but his gaze is warm and honest.

"If I say it, will you decide to trust me?"

"I already trust you. Really, Ada. The problem is more everybody else."

"You're talking about the hole in the fence," I say. My heart starts drumming crazily, just from hearing myself admit that much. "You're talking about how you leave the grounds whenever you want, even though we're all supposed to be locked up here. And if the people outside ever saw you swimming around free, they would smash down the gate for real and kill as many of us as they could."

I almost say that he must have some huge reason to put us all at risk like that or he would never do it, but I stop myself. I'm not about to mention anything about his pet sea monster, either.

Rowan stares into my eyes for a while, looking for anything I'm still hiding. I gaze straight back. I'm better prepared this time, and after a few moments, he nods.

"I honestly don't worry too much about anyone out there noticing me. When I'm in the water you have to get right up in my face to know I'm not a seal, and I don't let that happen. What are you, forty-five, forty-six? I'm only, like, forty-one. *Seal* is a big part of me. I want to make sure you really understand that."

I can make out the wall now, the gray stones shining through the trees up ahead. I probably shouldn't blame Rowan —I wasn't going to find whatever it is anyway, not without the blue here to guide me—but the sight of that wall weighs on me. It's hard not to feel like a failure. A few white birch trees gleam like searchlights behind him.

"Seals are awesome," I say, but I'm not really focused on him now. "It's one of the best animals you could get. I have no idea what I am."

"Ms. Stuart thinks you might be part mantis shrimp. Even though they're not native here. One could have escaped from an aquarium, maybe."

It takes a second for that to get through to me, but when it does, I almost fall over. The ground seems unstable here, somehow. "Part *shrimp?*"

"*Mantis* shrimp. And they're actually really cool," Rowan starts to say. "They—"

Beneath my feet the earth gives way. Rowan shouts and lunges for my arm, and misses, but his momentum sends him stumbling forward. I go skidding on my back down a steep slope covered in rocks that roll away whenever I grab at them. Rowan is right behind me, flailing. He accidentally kicks me in the face.

I land hard with all the breath knocked out of me. I barely manage to fling myself out of Rowan's way, and he still thumps down on my legs. Then we're both lying panting in a twilit cave. Light filters from the hole we fell through and rebounds off the craggy walls around us.

"Ada? You're okay?"

"I think just bruised. Plus you're crushing my calves." He gives a half laugh and heaves himself off me. "How about you?"

"Bruised. The fur helps some."

The light isn't just coming from outside. And it's a touch too blue to be daylight.

Several yards away from us, there's a dip in the cave's floor, and something in there is glowing.

Rowan notices how my attention has turned away from him. "Ada? Do you *see* something over there?" He squints. "It's so dark back there. I can't see anything. You seriously can?"

"It's not that dark for me." I get up, stiff from how banged up I am, and walk over. There's an irregular pool sunk into the stone, maybe five feet across and three feet deep. The blue is crumpled up beneath the glassy surface as if it were sleeping. Its glow floods the water up to the brim, and passing quivers cast webs of shine onto the walls.

But the blue isn't all that's in there.

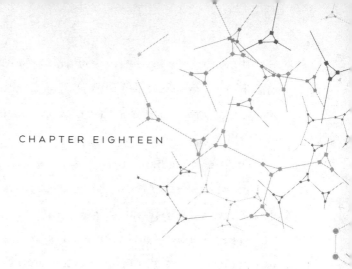

CHAPTER EIGHTEEN

T
HIS IS it. This is what the blue wanted me to see. Somebody — Ms. Stuart? Dr. Jacoway? — must be in the middle of a horrible experiment. Just like the blue said, they want power, though I can't begin to imagine what they're planning to do with the things in the pool. There are dozens of them, all jostling and slithering over one another, their skins various shades of waxy yellow and whitish green. They look more or less like insanely oversize tadpoles, but their faces are human, scrunched like the faces of just-born babies, and the legs starting to emerge by their tails end in tiny human feet. There are swollen purplish dots where their eyes should be; maybe they haven't opened yet.

I can't hold back a shriek, and Rowan comes stumbling over, stubbing his toes on rocks that seem obvious to me. "Ada? What is it?"

What can I say to him? Rowan is so sweet and easygoing

that it's really hard to remember how dangerous it might be to trust him. I can never tell him about the blue, for one thing, or what it mouthed at me. He probably wouldn't understand why I think Ms. Stuart wanting power could be a problem.

On the other hand, if he starts fumbling around in the pool or carries one of those things back to the light, he'll find out for himself what made me scream.

"There's some kind of kimes in there," I say. Now that I'm over being startled, I kneel down to watch them, and Rowan fumbles a hand to my shoulder and kneels next to me. "But not like us. Not nearly as — human."

Rowan stares down intensely. "My eyes are adjusting. I can see things moving. Do you think I'll hurt one if I pick it up?"

That's why I can't help liking him, even if he is spying on me — because that's the first thing he thinks about.

"Maybe it's okay for a few seconds? They're like tadpoles. They shouldn't be out of the water for long."

Rowan nods. "I just want to see. If we had a flashlight I'd never disturb them. But I kind of have to know what we're dealing with."

I don't want to risk him touching the blue. It's a weird sensation, more like a buzzing field than like solid matter, and he'll definitely wonder what's going on. "Let me do it. I can see them better. You might hurt one by accident."

I have to brace myself to reach in there. The creatures look slimy and pitiful, their gooey little feet kicking at each other as they swim. The instant my fingers graze the water, they start writhing frantically, trying to get away, their mouths opening and closing in silent, fishy fear.

As gently as I can, I catch one just under its tiny arms and lift it. It feels as awful as I expected, and its heartbeat patters into my fingers. It flinches violently at the touch of air. Once it's out of the water, we can both hear the noise it's making: a long, wheezy, barely there squeal.

"It's terrified." I hold it in the direction of the filtering daylight. "Rowan, can you see? Can I put it back?"

"Barely." He looks sick, his face working like he's about to cry. "Oh, Ada, just let it go! I'm sorry I asked!"

I lower it into the water and it splashes away, burrowing under its friends. A droplet splashes on my lip, and the taste is sharp with salt. I would have expected fresh water for things this froggy. "I'm sorry," I tell them, though I'm pretty sure there isn't enough human in them for language to mean anything. "Rowan, I could describe them for you?"

"I got the idea." Considering the kids we live with, and what we are ourselves, I never would have expected Rowan to sound so squeamish. "Ugh. Well, I guess it stands to reason."

"What stands to reason?"

"Oh — that if there are mostly human chimeras, there could also be chimeras that go the other way. Ones that are mostly animal, with pieces of *us* mixed in. Right, Ada? But those — I don't know, they're still little, but I don't get the feeling that they're even conscious beings. They don't seem any smarter than worms, or frogs. It's like seeing what we are, but dragged down." He shudders.

So that's what's bothering him. He wants to believe that kimes are a glorious improvement on regular humans, and these seem like such sad, helpless creatures. They'll probably have a worse chance of surviving than they would if they were ordinary tadpoles, even. Their feet aren't as good for swimming, for one thing.

The blue nestles itself around them. Tenderly, like a living blanket. What is it doing in there?

"So how do you think they got here?" I ask carefully — because I'm pretty sure someone must have created them on purpose, but why? If you wanted to grow a kime army, those tadpole things don't look like they'd make the greatest soldiers.

"Say you're right about the parasitic algae, like you told Dr. Jacoway? Then algae that were carrying human chromosomes infected a frog, and she laid her eggs in this pool, and that's what happened when the eggs hatched."

It sounds almost reasonable when he says it like that. "You think they just happened by accident?" I don't know why I have such a strong sense that an accident had nothing to do with it — that these creatures were made deliberately. And if these guys can live in salt water, they must be something more complicated than just a mix of frog and human genes. I don't really know, but putting together creatures with that much complexity seems to me like maybe *signs of intelligence,* all over again.

"Well, sure." He seems surprised that it's even a question. "We're all accidents. And I guess the thing about that is that some accidents turn out a lot better than others." He chokes up a sound that isn't quite a laugh. "See, Ada? This is why you shouldn't worry about us being contagious. Even though I bet we're *not*."

"What—because if we go around spreading Chimera Syndrome, really fabulous beings like these creepy tadpoles will happen? Rowan, I'm, uh, not sure that's logical."

"Ada, think about it! You talked about us coming from super-powerful algae. So where's the algae?"

Now I get it. "In the ocean."

"So Chimera Syndrome won't need us to spread! The whole business of locking us up and putting Long Island under quarantine—it's all just for show! The government has no idea how to stop it from spreading, so they're playing this stupid game to keep everyone calm. But the reality is, it's just a matter of time. They can't control the whole ocean. You see?"

"Unless that algae went extinct a year or two after it got out of Novasphere, and ever since Chimera Syndrome has been spread by people like me! If it was spreading through the ocean, it would be all over the place by now. What would stop it?"

Rowan shakes his head disapprovingly. "You're so smart, and you just use your brains to make yourself feel guilty. It's too bad." He gives me a long stare, probably straining to make out my expression in the dimness. "It's *really* too bad. But it doesn't seem like you'll let me talk you out of it."

"You're right, I won't. Because I don't want to lie to myself, Rowan. So how do we get out of here?" We scramble to our feet and turn toward the rubble where we slid down. The slope back up to the surface is only maybe ten feet or so tall, but the rocks are loose, and there's not a whole lot else to hold on to.

We walk back there and look it over. "If you climb on my shoulders, maybe you could grab those roots?" Rowan points. "I bet you could pull yourself up from there."

"Then what about you?"

"I'll wait while you go get help," he says, and then stops abruptly. "Or—we were going to tell Ms. Stuart about this, right?"

I guess I have to say it. "And what if she's totally aware of this place? What if this is one of those things I'm not supposed to know about, like that hole in the fence? I don't need her to be any weirder about me than she is already."

Rowan gets one of his thoughtful looks. "I guess that's a possibility. Okay. Then you didn't see it. I'm the only one who fell down here, and you—you're pretty dirty, so we have to say something—you tried to pull me out, and when you couldn't, you ran back to the hotel. Sound good?"

It sounds good if he sticks to our story. It sounds good, unless he's planning to betray me. I look in his face, and it seems kind and honest and open, and I just don't know whether to trust him. But I can't think of a better idea.

"Okay."

He crouches down and braces himself against the wall of scree while I clamber onto his shoulders and plant my feet as securely as I can. His fur and the softness of his flesh make it kind of precarious. He stands slowly, leaning forward into the slope for balance, and I straighten myself and reach for the looping roots. I grab the lowest one and yank; it's strong.

"You've got it, Ada?"

"I've got it." I heave myself up with all my strength, and Rowan helps by grabbing my sneakers and pushing up from below. Once I get a knee on the roots, it's easier. I manage to pull my torso up onto the forest floor, then after kicking for a few seconds, I swing my legs around onto solid ground, too. I get to my feet and look down at Rowan's round pink face, turned up to me. The sun is sinking at the perfect angle to frame him in a brilliant splotch of gold. "Thank you. I'll be back as soon as I can, okay?"

"I'm not going anywhere." He smiles. "Hey, Ada?"

"What?" I see something in his face, but I can't quite put my finger on it. Maybe *wistful* is the right word?

"Never mind. But thanks for not being too mad at me, about the spying. I would absolutely never do anything that could hurt you. I wouldn't even think it. You know that?"

"Not really," I tell him. "I don't *know* anything. But I want to believe that we're friends."

"We're friends," he says, but there's an ironic tension in his voice that makes me a little uncomfortable. "I'll see you soon."

It seems like there's something else I should say, maybe even something important, but I'm not sure what it is. So I wave to him and take off. It must be dinnertime by now, and everyone will be wondering where we are.

There's so much I have to figure out, but the whole time I'm running back through the woods and across the meadow, I can't keep my thoughts together. Instead my mind is just a big mess of images: those part-human tadpoles, Rowan's face gazing up from the hole, and the spilled blood on the Novasphere parking lot, beaming with sunlight, that Dr. Jacoway talked about.

And the blue just now, folding itself into a nest. The blue last night, pretending to be me, and a spinning globe, and then me all over again.

CHAPTER NINETEEN

T

WENTY MINUTES later, Ms. Stuart and Dr. Jacoway, Gabriel and Martin—who is also thirteen and part beetle, with useless iridescent green wings and antennae and disturbing extra joints in his arms and legs, and who seems pretty seriously not bright—are all following me through the woods. Gabriel has a coil of rope slung from one shoulder and a flashlight sticking out of his left pocket. Furious jags of color are running through his skin, even though I've told him five times that Rowan is fine. I'm not sure I've ever seen him this tense.

"Ada? You said it was in sight of the wall?" Ms. Stuart asks after we've been wandering back and forth for a while. "You're sure about that?"

I bet she knows exactly where it is. Why do we have to go through this charade of searching everywhere? "I noticed the wall through the trees, but it wasn't that close. And there was a clump of paper birch trees maybe twenty feet away, in the direction of the water."

"The birches!" Dr. Jacoway exclaims. "Five of them, arching gracefully outward like the jets of a fountain? Pearl-colored in the gloom?"

I think there were five trunks, now that I hear him say it. "That's probably right. Do you know where they are?"

"I do, I do. A favored spot of mine, on those rare occasions when I can steal a solitary hour. Not that I regret any of it, not a single moment of the years I've devoted to you children. You are my heart's refuge. The only beings I have ever seen both strange and revelatory enough to make me feel truly at home . . ." His head starts rocking and I get a little worried that he's completely forgotten what we're doing out here, but then he snaps into focus again. "Come. We are much too far from the sea."

He turns and plunges in a waddling way into an especially dense patch of underbrush, cracking and stamping, and we all go after him.

"Rowan?" Gabe yells. "Rowan? Where are you?"

A responding cry, or maybe a moan, echoes dimly through the trees. If that's Rowan, he must have been badly injured somehow in the time I've been away. I thought Gabriel was overreacting, but now urgency jolts through me, too.

"Rowan, we're here! We're coming!"

It's getting darker, orange slices of sunset stretching ahead as we walk. In the dusk the birches stand out like arms reaching up for us.

The moaning sound comes again, but this time it seems much too far away to be coming from anywhere near those trees. "Gabe? Do you think that's him?" I ask. "I thought at first it was, but now it sounds wrong."

Gabriel just shakes his head without looking at me. It's like he thinks this is my fault. I feel like snapping at him that Rowan was the one following *me*, not the other way around.

"Careful, please," Dr. Jacoway murmurs. "Gabriel, you are too impetuous. We can't have you falling in as well, not when you're carrying the rope." He chuckles, so maybe that was his idea of a joke. All at once he veers left and drops to his knees, staring at the ground. Once I get there I can see how Rowan and I broke through a tangle of thin branches and vines on our way into that underground pit; maybe someone deliberately concealed the entrance. "Rowan, my dear boy, are you down there?" Dr. Jacoway shouts down, then cocks his head and listens. "Isn't this the place?"

He's asking Gabriel; probably he's completely forgotten who I am again.

"This is it. Definitely. Isn't Rowan there?" I drop down next to Dr. Jacoway. The sun has sunk low enough that not a single beam makes it into the pit, and as far as I can tell, the blue has gone, too. All I see is shadow. Maybe Rowan fell asleep so far back in the cave that I can't see the glow of his warmth? "Rowan? Rowan, it's me, Ada! We're here to get you out!"

Ms. Stuart just stands there with a strange look on her face. With the sun falling behind her, it's hard to figure out what she's feeling.

That moaning yowl blasts through the woods again, and now I'm positive it can't be Rowan. It's deep and rumbling, but with a piercing, tinny warble at the top. It's coming from the direction of the sea, and there's no imaginable whale song or seal bark that could sound like that. A shiver crawls down my back.

The weird thing is that Gabriel isn't bent over the ragged roots framing the hole, screaming for his missing friend. He's standing five feet away with his hands on his hips, staring into the distance where we all heard that cry.

I try not to, but I start imagining what it could be. I saw the kimes in the pool. If there are other mostly animal kimes out here, some of them might be a lot bigger. A lot more vicious. Maybe that bellowing thing came ashore and reached into the hole with endless, many-segmented arms while Rowan gaped up at it, too petrified to run. Or maybe it crawled in from the darkness and throttled him before he even saw it. Now that I think about it, I didn't notice a back wall in the shadows past the pool.

"We have to go down there! The cave—Rowan said it went back—it might turn into a tunnel. We have to look for him."

Ms. Stuart raises an eyebrow. "Are you volunteering, Ada?"

Gabriel definitely told her everything I said about the blue, because for the first time it's obvious how much she dislikes me.

"I'd—rather not go alone. But even with the flashlight,

the rest of you might miss Rowan in the dark somewhere, and I won't. I mean, if he was knocked unconscious somehow." Of course, if those tadpole things in the pool are Ms. Stuart's experiment, she'll probably find an excuse to keep me out of the cave. She'll want only people she trusts to see them. "So yes, I'm volunteering."

Unless she knows exactly what's making that cry. It could be another one of her special projects. Maybe she's so fed up with me that she'll send me down there knowing I won't come back.

She gives me a nod, but her mouth stays grim. If the tadpoles aren't *her* creation, then who else could be responsible? Dr. Jacoway is just too out of it, I think.

"No one could say that you lack for courage, Ada. We can use the rope to lower you first. I'll follow. Gabriel and Dr. Jacoway should wait here."

Gabriel whirls on her. "I am *not* waiting! Ada can sit around while we go search for Rowan. Ms. Stuart, if *she's* getting—I mean, you know it's serious. Rowan wouldn't just run off into some tunnel when he knew we were coming."

"She?" I ask. No one answers. I don't think he was talking about me, though.

"Ada raised a compelling point. This is precisely the kind of situation where her abilities can be most useful to us."

"Then *you* wait here. Ada and I will go. What, are you worried that I'll lose her for you?" Gabriel might be rude to everyone else, but I'm not used to hearing him talk to Ms. Stuart this way; she and Rowan are the only two people I'd guess he genuinely loves. More than anything that's happened so far, the snapping shows how agitated Gabe really is.

So what was he about to say? *If she's getting angry? If she's getting hungry?* Could *she* mean that long, rippling serpent shape I saw out in the ocean?

"The last time you and Ada undertook a mission together, Gabriel, it didn't turn out especially well. I don't doubt your commitment. Your judgment is another matter."

Gabriel grins harshly. "It turned out great, actually. We haven't had any more trouble with normals screaming at the gate since then. What happened that night must have really freaked them out."

Ms. Stuart might hate me, but not enough to be happy with Gabe basically saying that getting me bashed in the head was a fantastic idea. She gives me a quick, embarrassed look.

"What about me?" Martin asks sleepily. "I'm stronger than any of you." His antennae twitch. No one answers.

Gabe smirks, pivots away from us, and flings himself down into the hole. The rocks rattle under his body, and he crashes with a gasp. It takes me a moment to realize that he carried the rope in there with him, so there's no chance of anyone else getting lowered down gently, either. Whoever goes is going the hard way.

"I'm okay," he calls up. I can see him down there in the dark, a red shape hunched on the rocks. He's clutching his ankle.

"Gabriel!" Ms. Stuart yells fiercely. "Gabriel, forcing the issue is in no way acceptable behavior. Get—" Then she realizes how absurd it is to order him to climb back up here. That's why he took the rope with him: so there would be no choice. She snorts and turns to me. "Ada? Are you still volunteering to go, even though your companion is clearly a reckless idiot?"

From something in the tone of her voice, I know she's angry in the way parents get when they're very afraid for you. Out of all the kids here, Gabriel is the one she truly loves as her own son.

"I'm still volunteering," I say. "Rowan is my friend too."

Her eyebrows contract just a bit. "In the outside world, adults have the luxury of being precious about the safety of children. We don't have that here. All we have are common resources and calculations as to how best to use what we have. For Rowan's sake, I would stake a great deal. We are using you now, Ada: using your abilities to find a boy we all love. I want to make sure that's clear."

"You aren't using me," I snap. It's hard to face slamming into that hole again, but I shift myself and sit on the edge. "I'm not going to find Rowan for you. I'm using *myself* to help someone I care about."

She smiles. "By all means, think of it that way. If you prefer."

I don't say anything, just push off with both hands. The darkness opens around me like a wound, and the rocks clamor and jump at my back. I wasn't prepared for how much sliding down would hurt now that I'm already bruised. I land in a swirl of bouncing stones and skid five feet before my body wheels to a halt.

Gabriel's got the flashlight out. He's aiming it into the pool. His right knee is bent like he's trying to keep his weight off that ankle.

I stand up, stiff and aching, and walk back to the bottom of the hole. "Ms. Stuart? We're all right. We'll come back as soon as we find him."

"We'll be waiting, Ada. Try to restrain Gabriel's more foolish impulses, if that's possible." She's bending over, her head and shoulders a ruby blotch against the fraying trees.

"Who on earth is that girl?" Dr. Jacoway asks. His voice sounds dim and shaky. "She seemed to materialize out of purest nothingness, but somehow I have the strangest feeling that I've seen her somewhere before."

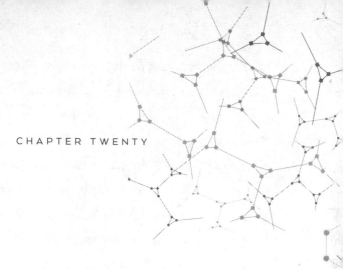

CHAPTER TWENTY

GABRIEL SWINGS the beam across my face. "Don't look at me like that. I didn't do anything that dumb. We can throw the rope up to them once we've got him."

I nod at his ankle. Now that I'm standing here on aching legs, I'm not sure why I didn't tell Ms. Stuart that he'd hurt himself, except that I knew he didn't want me to. "It's pretty dumb to mess yourself up before we even start searching." I keep my voice just above a whisper. "It's not broken, is it?"

"Sprained. So walking on it will hurt." Gabe shrugs. "I'll deal."

"Oh, that'll work great. Until we have to carry Rowan out of here. As long as we don't have to run." He heard that thing moaning as well as I did.

He's still standing right by the pool, and I keep waiting for him to freak out about those tadpole creatures. He seems awfully casual for just having seen something that disturbing—unless, of course, he already knew all about them. I walk up to him and he doesn't move, not even when I tug the flashlight out of his hand. The first thing I do is point the light toward the darkness beyond the pool, searching for where Rowan might have gone. Sure enough, there's a rounded spot on the wall where the darkness sinks deeper than the beam can reach. Then I comb the light across all the corners, just to make extra sure he's not here, though I don't see body heat coming from anywhere but the two of us.

It's only then that I let myself shine the light down into the glassy stillness of that water, greenish black now that the blue isn't there to illuminate it.

It's empty. I swing the beam back and forth across the pool, trying to be casual about it. There are a few jags of rock below the surface, but they aren't nearly big enough to hide that crowd of writhing human-faced kimes. The green glass skin hovers over emptiness, algae, a single lost snail. I'm pretty sure those tadpole things couldn't have slithered off on their own and found a new pool to live in; the one I picked up shrank desperately from the air. But who could have moved them?

Even stranger: the level of the water is a lot lower now. A blackish stain rims the rocks ten inches above the surface, showing how high the pool was only an hour ago.

"I was hoping that pool might be a way through to the sea," Gabe says morosely. "Rowan can stay under for longer than you can imagine."

I can't react, not with Gabriel watching me. I point toward the deepening black on the wall again. "That way, then.

There's nowhere else he could have gone." Gabriel reaches for the flashlight, but I ignore him and walk forward with as much determination as I can manage. Gabriel's stuck tagging after me, and for a moment I'm glad about that.

At least, I'm glad until we hear that moaning howl again. It's much louder down here, echoing off the walls until we're caught in a barrage of repeating cries like a thousand broken voices all pelting in on us.

Whatever it is making that sound, it's straight ahead.

The tunnel descends unevenly and also gets narrower. It's rough going: a natural fissure, not something people made or smoothed out. The ceiling is too high to touch. What was Rowan thinking? It seems impossible that he just walked off this way deliberately. It's hard enough not to bash against blades of cracked rock even with the flashlight, and he would have had to pass this way in utter dark. I keep searching the peaked stones for any sign of him: if something dragged him through here, wouldn't there be scraps of his clothes that snagged and tore?

Wouldn't there be blood?

Where is the blue now that I desperately need its help? It was down here with Rowan when I left. Wouldn't it know what happened to him?

The walls squeeze in and Gabriel pants behind me, suppressing tiny gasps of pain each time his right foot touches down. Our warmth casts a red quiver on the walls and sends ragged shadow shapes flapping ahead of us. The space is so tight now that I have to turn sideways and shimmy through a gap, but when I point the flashlight up, its beam lances endlessly into blackness, touching nothing but pinwheeling bats.

As we twist around a corner, there's a new sound: a deep, dreamy booming. The voice cries out again, and now it sounds so close that I jump and wave the flashlight ahead of me. The light skitters and tears on the ragged stones.

And then reflects off a pair of eyes maybe two feet above the floor. They're staring straight into mine. A rocky crest blocks the lower half of the face from view.

Those eyes seem human, or they would if there were human beings with eyes ten inches across and even farther apart. Green-golden, the same color as mine, set in grayish skin with a damp shine to it. Their lashes are as heavy as black tusks. There's no glow of warmth: that creature is cold through and through. Something thicker than hair spills back behind what I guess is a forehead the size of a dresser. I don't have long to look, but I get the feeling that whatever it is there in the dark knows exactly who I am, and that it bitterly resents me — and maybe it feels something else, too, though I can't put my finger on what.

There's a shuddering groan, a splash, and then the creature is gone. I don't have to walk over there to know that we've found a passage through to the sea. The truth is that I'd be way too scared to get any closer.

Behind me, Gabriel hasn't made a single sound, but it's like I can feel his tension drawn all over my back in black marker. I turn to him with the flashlight aimed at his chest, though I'd rather shine it straight in his face.

"That was *she*," I say. "Wasn't it? The *she* you started talking about before. So who is she?"

Gabriel hesitates. "You're the one who needs to start answering questions, Ada. It's just plain stupid for you to try asking them. It's a lot dumber than anything *I've* done. What are we supposed to think, when you're so nosy?"

I guess I should be worried. Gabriel could shove me into the gap that monster came out of, and nobody would ever know. But I'm shaking all over with something a lot colder and wilder than fear, and I don't care what he does.

"What did she do to Rowan?"

He scowls. "You know too much already."

"I've *seen* her, Gabriel! How am I supposed to keep from knowing about things I've seen for myself? Do you not even care if that thing strangled your friend?"

"Of course I care! But Soraya loves Rowan, okay? She would never hurt him. Unless—"

He stops, brows drawn, and chews his lip. Violent slants of color collide all over his skin. And he's glaring at me like, whatever happened to Rowan, it's definitely my fault.

I don't want to understand why that creature—Soraya? —looked at me the way she did, but all at once I get it. I never tried to make Rowan like me. It didn't even cross my mind until just now that he might.

Rowan never actually *said* that those tadpole creatures

were the first mostly animal kimes he'd seen, but I feel my heart contracting just a little with the realization of how totally he's been deceiving me. I guess we're even, but I still feel betrayed.

Gabriel hasn't taken his eyes off me once, but suddenly he's three steps closer.

"Ms. Stuart is convinced we need you. She thinks you could be the key to the whole thing, if you actually cared about being on our side. She thinks you could help us control the power that's here, even if you're pretending now you don't know what I'm talking about. But I don't think you're ever going to be that useful. It's like you have some kind of delusion that your parents will want you back if you keep sticking up for the normals. It's pathetic, Ada. You could be part of something new and amazing, something that could change the whole world, and instead you're clinging to the past like all the other losers."

He's getting in my face, and I start to back away—but maybe ten paces behind me there's the opening where Soraya was peering out at us. She might still be lurking just below the water's surface, and for all I know, that surface is a long way down.

"Gabriel, what are you doing?"

"You should really start talking, Ada. You should do whatever it takes to make us care what happens to you. In case you haven't noticed, we're all you have now."

The air around us shakes with the hollow boom of the sea. I can't let Gabe keep herding me toward that hole in the floor, so I stop with my legs apart and braced. He's a lot bigger than I am, but he's also injured.

"Are you seriously about to try and murder me?" I'm straining to sound contemptuous, but my voice jumps.

"Soraya wouldn't kill Rowan, I don't think, not even if she is pissed off with him. But maybe she hid him somewhere. Maybe I can trade you to get him back. Since you're the one she *really* hates. It won't be me murdering you, though. Not technically." He shoves me with a queasy grin plastered on his face, and I stumble three steps deeper into the cave. "Tell me everything you've seen since you came here. Tell me you'll persuade your blue thing to help us—to break through whatever the problem is that's been holding back our project. It'll know exactly what I mean. Then I might decide we need you after all."

There's a good chance he's bluffing. This might even be something he and Ms. Stuart planned together, to scare me into spilling my secrets. Though, now I think about it, I don't know when they would have had a chance to come up with a plot like that. We all left right after I ran into the dining room yelling that Rowan was trapped.

"Do you really think Rowan would forgive you for helping to kill me? You'll lose your best friend."

Gabriel grins. All the wild ripping colors have drained from his skin. He's icy white, cold and calm and determined, and seeing that floods me with shivers. My knees are starting to buckle under me, and when he slams me again, I totter back hard. My calves smack into a low wall of rock. I nearly tip backwards, and my arms fly out, wheeling at the emptiness for a terrible moment before I find my balance again. It must be the rock that half hid Soraya's face.

That means I'm on the brink. Dank air breathes up the back of my shirt, bringing a reek of iron and salt and clay. Even without looking behind me, I can feel how deep and cavernous that vacancy is. I can already sense what it will be like to fall: the stone throat swallowing me, the crash into cold waves. And then Soraya, whatever she is, and her hatred for me.

"Rowan won't have to know. I'll say you had an accident. Talk, Ada. Now. Because I'm getting bored of waiting."

I have exactly one chance. If I mess up, he'll probably fling me over the edge in a rage. He reaches up and grabs my shoulders, his fingers digging into the bruises on my back.

If he sees me glance down, he'll be ready for me. I keep my eyes fixed on his and silently lift my left foot, then kick his hurt ankle as hard as I can. He grunts and his right leg gives way beneath him. The flashlight drops and rolls away across the ground, flinging up mountains of shadow as it goes.

I was planning to leap over him and go sprinting back up the tunnel, but he keeps his grip on my shoulders and I can't twist free. Instead I go toppling down with him and land sprawled on his chest. I lash out at his bad ankle again, pounding viciously in the hope that the pain will make him let go, but he's as determined as I am, and, locking one arm around my head, he throws me onto my side.

Then something wet and gummy, and as thick as a human thigh, snakes around my left arm. There's something horrible mixed into the sensation of the wetness, as if a hundred rasping mouths were chewing on me.

For maybe half a second I find myself hanging in midair, looking down into Gabe's shocked face, traced along one side by the flashlight's beam. More snaking things are holding me now. It's all happening so fast that I can't make sense of any of it.

"Where's Rowan?" Gabe screams. "You can have Ada, I don't care! Give back Rowan!"

Soraya. What *is* she?

Then I'm arching through the darkness. The ocean gulps me down.

CHAPTER TWENTY-ONE

I'M TRAPPED in freezing, tearing, watery blackness. Flashes of my own red warmth shine between her coils, but I can't see anything else. My chest gets tighter and tighter, yearning for air, but we must be in some flooded tunnel deep in solid stone. My whole body heaves with the urge to breathe. She's going to drown me, and that's it.

A huge face looms into mine. A mouth bigger than a bucket opens and swallows my entire head; rubbery lips seal tight around my neck. I'm gagging from the stink of it, like fish and wet pennies, and from the sharp blast of humid air.

Air. My lungs open, and I start panting and coughing inside Soraya's vast mouth. She's sharing her air with me on purpose, and it makes no sense. She was moments away from getting rid of me for good and having Rowan all to herself again. Her moaning thrums in my eardrums until my head sings with pain, but I'm still alive and rushing at a crazy speed through the water. I can't tell how much time is passing; the moments rumble along for what might be minutes or hours.

Blue stars shine in the blackness of her mouth. I'm reeling with an impossible dizziness, vomit rising and retreating in my throat. My legs burn with shocking pain, and after a few moments, I realize it's the salt getting into all my scratches.

Then she spits me out. I look out at a field of dusky waves, a final ribbon of sunset still caught at the sky's back edge. I can see the lights of the Genesis Institute gleaming on the hill, but we're a long way out. "Soraya," I gasp. I'm sure Gabe is right. She hates me with a passion. So why am I alive? "Thank you."

Her tentacles twist me around, and I stare into a single giant eye. Those rasping mouths all over my body are her suckers. She's so big that I can see only a few slices of her looming from the water, but I see enough to get an idea. Her head is bald and slick and maybe earless, a cascade of heavy tentacles spiraling back from her forehead.

She's a kime, of course. Part human, part giant squid?

She pulls me back twenty feet and lifts her head out of the water down to her chin. She looks horribly sad, and long, groaning breaths squeeze through her lips. The sight of her whole face races through me.

I've never seen anyone who looks so completely like me, not even my mom.

All her features are enormous: eyes like molten olive glass, a nose as long as my forearm, gray-blue lips like ocean waves. But every detail is shaped exactly, precisely, the same as it is on me, just crazily inflated. The look in her eyes is heavy with a disturbing, lonely intelligence. I'm sure she can understand me.

Apart from her grayish skin and her monstrous size and those tentacles, we could be identical twins.

Maybe we are. A kind of twins, anyway. Maybe some of the algae that infected me when my mom was pregnant copied a chunk of my DNA and carried it into Soraya when she was just starting to form. And I get a chilly understanding of why she might resent me: not just because Rowan likes me, but because he maybe likes me for being a more human version of *her*.

"Hi," I say. "I'm really not trying to take Rowan away from you. I mean, if that's something you're worried about? Can—do you speak English?"

Her voice rattles in response. Her mouth looks human, but maybe she doesn't have all the right parts inside for speech.

"Do you know where Rowan is?" She didn't take him; I know that now. I don't think Gabe understands her at all. She was never planning to kill me, either. The more I look at her, the more certain I feel that she really is my sister, and that she knew it way before I did.

Her voice is still wordless, but I can hear the anxiety bubbling through it. She pivots her eyes across the sea and howls. That's what she's been doing: she's calling him, just like we were.

"If you didn't take him, what did? He knew we were

coming for him. He wouldn't want to scare us by disappearing like that."

Soraya gives a startled yelp and swings me around, facing me back toward the beach and shaking me. We're far enough away that I can barely make it out: a reddish shape crawling out of the sea and onto the deserted beach. Then it stops, clinging to the sand in an exhausted-looking heap.

"Rowan! Soraya, is that him?"

She looks at me wide-eyed as if she's about to cry, then her mouth engulfs my head again. We dive with a violent rippling motion that sends my stomach reeling.

A minute or so later, I feel my body abruptly released and flying through the water so fast I have to fight an impulse to scream. My head splits the water's surface, but foam flies at my face, so I keep my lids closed. There's a clang, and my hands fly out and grip the wires of our chain link fence.

I open my eyes and gape around. I'm on the inside of our penned-in piece of ocean, breathless and rocking with the waves. The sea is much rougher than usual, and salt slaps into my mouth. My hair is clumped with Soraya's sticky, fishy saliva.

But I'm pretty sure that shape sprawled on the beach is Rowan. He's alive, and so am I, and, no matter how she feels about me, Soraya saved my life.

From Gabriel. Will anyone believe me if I tell them what he did? Ophelia's crazy about him, Rowan is his best friend, and Ms. Stuart thinks of him as her own kid. And who am I to any of them?

The new girl. The one who's a little too human. The one they've never really trusted.

I clutch the fence, dreading the swim back. I wonder if Gabriel's gone back up the tunnel already, tossing up the rope. I wonder if they've pulled him out and he's walking home through the woods, telling some smug story of how I slipped and fell and there was nothing he could do.

Part of me wants to swim as fast as I can to Rowan, but I can't. I need to decide what to say before I face any of them. The truth hits me as if all my blood had frozen at once: if I get this wrong, if I make a mistake, I'll have another "accident" in no time. There's no good solution that I can see, but maybe I can at least buy myself some time if I do the opposite of whatever Gabriel is expecting. I can't count on Soraya being there to save me again.

Soraya. I hope she believed what I told her about Rowan. I would never want to hurt her. Never.

We're family.

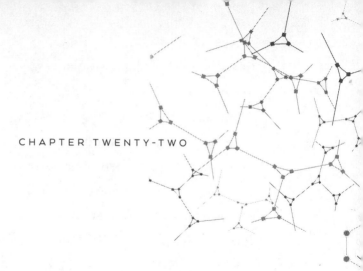

CHAPTER TWENTY-TWO

W HEN I REACH the shore, Rowan is still there, sprawled face-down with his T-shirt soaked and sticking to his fur, and his wide, fur-topped feet bare on the sand. He must have lost his shoes when he was swimming. I have a flash of fear for him—why hasn't he run back to the hotel?—but his warmth is still bright, and his back is heaving. I shuffle over to him on my knees, my drowned clothes streaming water with each soggy movement, and reach to touch his shoulder. He's shaking; he's drenched, and a cool, harsh wind blares from the sea, but I didn't think he could get cold this easily.

"Rowan?"

He startles, and slowly turns a tear-streaked face to me. "Ada!" I see him taking in my dripping, saliva-slimed hair, my torn shirt. I sit beside him with my arms wrapped tight around my chest. I don't think she did it on purpose, but Soraya's suckers shredded my clothes in places. "How

—getting through that underwater passage—the fence—are you—"

I'm not sure what he's getting at. "My *sister* saved me. She brought me back here. And I think you know her."

Rowan spasms again, then laboriously heaves himself up to sit cross-legged on the sand. His eyes are red, and he reaches self-consciously to smear his tears away.

"You met Soraya." He sighs. "She's been asking to meet you. I told her it was a terrible idea, but I thought she might not listen to me. The second I saw your face, I knew this was going to be a big problem."

"*Asking* to meet me?" I say. Does she have some way of talking that I don't know about?

Rowan's shaking his head. His eyes look glazed, disoriented. "She saved you, though? Soraya? What—" He's twisting himself harder now, like he can clear his mind by force. "Oh, no. Oh, Ada. You went back underground, and when you couldn't find me you started searching the tunnel? And —you, even *you* didn't see that gap in the floor somehow, and you fell into the water?"

"That's what Gabriel is going to tell everyone," I say. "He's probably telling them that story right now."

Rowan's eyes go wide as he takes this in. "Ada!"

"And I'm going to go along with it. I'm going to repeat whatever Gabe says. I won't tell anybody else the truth except you, Rowan. I just need someone to know, in case he tries it again."

"He *wouldn't*, though! He knows Ms. Stuart thinks—"

"Gabe thinks she's wrong. He thinks I'm useless. And he thought maybe Soraya stole you, so he wanted to trade me to get you back. He threatened to throw me to her if I wouldn't tell him whatever it is that you're all so sure I know." I'm kind of shocked by how cold my voice sounds. Relentless. "He was convinced that Soraya would murder me for him. He was being stupid. That's not what she's like. She grabbed me just the way he wanted, but she did it to save me *from* him."

"Of course she wouldn't actually murder you! Okay, so the first time she saw you she said some pretty upsetting things, and I guess I did tell Gabe about that, but still. She was basically in shock. How could Gabe possibly—" And then he gets it. His cheeks flush crimson. "Hey, Soraya's kind of my sister, too. We've been close since we were both babies. We grew up together."

"I'm not sure she sees it like that."

Rowan doesn't answer out loud, but I can read the look he fires at me: *You don't need to give me an excuse, Ada. I know you'll never like me that way.*

It seems like a good time to change the subject. "So how did *you* get here, Rowan? Why didn't you wait for us? I get that swimming out of there is no problem for you, but that's no reason to scare everybody!"

He gets a strange look on his face. The sun is totally under now, but a film of moonlight covers the two of us and glints gray on the sand. It's a gibbous moon, fat and sleepy, balanced on the horizon.

"Would you believe me if I told you that I can't remember? That I had a blackout and found myself here with my memory totally wiped—everything from the moment you left me?" Rowan asks.

I think about it. It sounds a lot like what happened to me after I saw the blue mouthing, *They want power.* The truth is we have no idea what it's capable of doing. And what was it Gabriel said—they think I can make it help them with their *project?* Is that what Ophelia was so worried about? That maybe if I refused, Ms. Stuart would try to force me somehow?

"I believe you," I tell him. "It's no crazier than anything else that's been happening."

"Good," Rowan says decidedly. He flashes me an awful smile, slow and contorted. "Because that's what *I'm* going to tell everyone. Except for you. We're going to walk back up there and lie our faces off together."

I stare at him. "So what actually happened?"

Rowan locks his gaze on mine. "Do you really not know? Really, Ada?"

The blue. Did he *see* it somehow?

"I went and sat back by the pool, and it got darker and darker. And then—I felt something take hold of my hand. It was, I don't know, not as solid as a human hand. It had kind of a sizzling feeling, like there was a lot going on inside it. I couldn't see anything, but I knew, I knew for sure, that it was the thing Ms. Stuart has been searching for. The thing you've been keeping secret." His smile looks a lot sadder now. "I'm not mad. I mean, I didn't tell you about Soraya. I still wouldn't want you to know about her, honestly, if it was up to me to decide. Did you see that thing in the cave when we were both there?"

I can't answer that. Can I answer that? "I saw it. It was curled up around those kimes in the pool. Like it was cuddling them."

"The same blue thing you started telling Gabe and Ophelia about. After those creeps knocked you out."

He's not lilting it like a question. He's announcing it like he's known all along.

"Yes." My heart speeds into a twitchy, unsure beat. I'm probably making a huge mistake by admitting this to anyone.

"So why didn't you tell Ms. Stuart the truth?"

"The blue didn't want me to."

I expect Rowan to argue, but he nods. "I kind of got that message, too. I don't know how, though. Or why. But it felt like everything it was showing me was just for me, and it wanted me to keep my mouth shut. Anyway, it took me by the hand, and I felt like I had to trust it. I felt like it was someone I'd missed for a long time without knowing it, if that makes sense. So I let it lead me away, even though it was so dark that I was completely blind. And the really crazy thing? When I put out my other hand, I touched water. Water was floating ahead of me in this wobbly cloud. I could stick my fingers right in, and it was full of swimming animals. Those tadpole kimes, Ada."

I'm the one nodding now. "The tadpoles were gone when Gabe and I went down there."

"Yeah. I have no idea where they are now. I bet your blue

thing knew more people were coming and it wanted to move them somewhere safer."

There's a pause while I think about that. There's something in what Rowan is saying that makes me feel like I'd rather not talk about this anymore. "Why would it care about protecting them? Rowan, look, everybody's scared out of their minds about you. We should go up."

"We have to figure this out first. I mean, don't *you* have any ideas about what that blue thing is? We know it's intelligent, and we know it went out of its way to protect those tadpole kimes. It seems like it cares about us, too. So, think: something that's at least as smart as we are, and that worries about different species—what does that sound like to you?"

I think of the blue turning itself into a rolling mass of animal parts, all mixed up together. It was trying to communicate *something* by doing that.

Voices float down from the top of the hill. I look up, and there's a cluster of bodies up there. They're just starting to make their way down the slope. I guess Rowan is right: whatever we have to tell each other, we'd better say now. I still don't like it, though—and I'm not quite ready to tell him about the blue shape-shifting in the woods, even though I'm pretty sure that's something he'd be excited to learn.

"But, Rowan, if the blue led you away on purpose, where was it taking you?"

His lips pinch a little; he's probably annoyed that I asked a new question instead of answering his.

"It wanted to show me something." That sounds familiar.

"There are caves leading off from that underwater tunnel, Ada. It tugged on me until I jumped down into the crack in the floor, just *trusting* it that there was water down there, and that I'd find a way out, because I still couldn't see anything. It took me on — I guess you'd call it a tour. I'm probably the only one of us who could've stayed under long enough for it to do that."

It doesn't make any sense, but panic rushes through me the way it did in the woods that time — right before I turned and ran frantically from the blue as it gibbered its silent words at me. *Ada, darling. They want power.*

"How could you see anything? If it was pitch-dark — "

"The caves *weren't* dark, is the thing. Just the passage. The caves were blazing, and it was all so insanely beautiful. Some kind of bioluminescence was everywhere, all over the walls. Green and blue and white stars living on the rocks. And the whole time I was thinking how I could never show it to you — that you would drown — but that you'd see it in ways nobody else ever could. That wasn't all that was in there, either. Not — not even close. Ada, listen, I think I know what the blue thing is trying to tell us."

I open my mouth to ask the question he's expecting: *what?* But the truth is that I don't want to know. Not right now, anyway. I'm beyond exhausted, and all at once the cold wind sucking on my drenched clothes is getting to me. I feel shaky and feverish.

But then I'm saved from asking him anything, because some of the kids heading down the hill catch sight of us and start hollering. "Is that Rowan? Rowan! Rowan! And who's with him? It looks like—but Gabe said—how could she have gotten here? Rowan! Ada! Is that you?"

Rowan shoots me a rueful look and stands up. "It's us! We're right here!"

"But Gabe said Ada fell into a chasm! He said she vanished!"

"She did. Soraya rescued her." I wish Rowan hadn't told them that part, but realistically there's no other explanation that would work. "She's kind of stunned, but she's fine."

"Ada!" Ophelia screams. "I was so, so, so upset! I couldn't believe you were gone!" There's a stampede of running feet on the slope above us, and then Ophelia launches herself off the ragged shelf where the grass drops sharply to the sand. Her wings thrum into an opal blur, and she sails twenty yards through the air, her body lifting in a long arc across the night, and lands on me in a squealing tangle. "Oh, gross. What's that all over your hair?"

And then we're both half laughing and half crying, and I'm shocked by how relieved I feel to be back with her—and by how relieved I am that she cares.

Besides, what she did just now? That looked to me like more than just hovering. It wasn't all *that* far, maybe, but it was a lot farther and higher than I've ever seen her go before.

Ophelia almost flew.

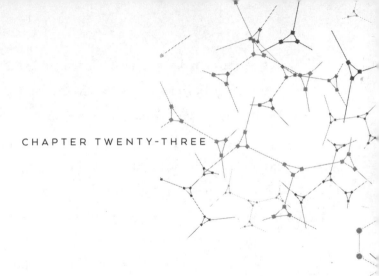

CHAPTER TWENTY-THREE

ONE OF the smaller kids there happens to have deer legs, and she drops to all fours and goes sprinting up the hill so fast I see her as a red blur weaving through the brambles. She's off to tell everybody that Rowan and I are safe, and that means I'll have to face Gabriel soon, but I barely bother to watch her run. Ophelia's still hugging me, and little Indigo is clinging to my right leg and crying, saying, "You couldn't be dead, you couldn't be, you couldn't, I won't ever let you die!" over and over again. I reach down to stroke her dusk blue cheeks, which don't sting.

Maybe a dozen kids are crowded around me and Rowan, and I stare out at the moon-speckled sea and let him do the talking. I don't like to think of Soraya out there by herself; wouldn't she rather be with all of us?

"It's really crazy," Rowan is saying. "I sat down in that cave to wait for Ada and Ms. Stuart to come back and rescue me, and—I guess I felt a *little* lightheaded, but I really thought

I was fine. Anyway I must have fainted, and when I came to I was at the edge of the water, right over there, feeling the sand suck out from under my hands. I have absolutely no idea how it happened. I was still catching my breath when Ada came crawling out of the sea and splatted down right beside me. I mean, there's obviously a tunnel through to the ocean in there, because that's how Soraya was able to save Ada. I must have gone through it, too."

Everyone's nodding. So they all knew about Soraya, but nobody told me. But do they know the really important thing?

"I couldn't believe how much she looks like me," I say, to check how everyone reacts.

"She does?" Ophelia sounds genuinely surprised, at least. She leans her head on my shoulder. "How *could* she look like you, though? Though I guess none of us but Rowan have ever seen her up close. She doesn't usually come — anywhere too near the fence — except to visit him. She's kind of a mysterious loner type. Soraya, lost princess of the whispering waves. Like that."

If Ophelia is telling the truth, then that explains why Rowan was the only one who really jumped when he first saw me.

But did Rowan truly keep that a secret even from Gabriel — that Soraya and I are obviously some kind of sisters? Maybe it makes a little more sense now that Gabe had such stupid ideas about her. He doesn't know her at all, and he just assumed she must be as cruel as he is.

"I mean, Soraya looks more like Ada than you'd expect,

considering she's mostly squid." Rowan's voice is lazy, but he flashes me a warning look over Ophelia's head. "I guess their eyes are similar. The same color, anyway."

"How did you get back over the fence?" someone asks.

"Soraya threw me over the top. I hit the water pretty hard. Maybe she threw Rowan, too, while he was unconscious? And I was facing the wrong way to see it?"

Rowan's aware that I know about the hole in the fence, but nobody else has to realize that. He beams at me, to let me know I said the right thing.

They're coming. A long trail of bodies like hazy red torches dots the hillside. I imagine how Gabriel must be practicing the words in his mind as he walks toward us: *Ada's crazy, she's lying, she's not one of us . . .* He can *almost* count on everyone believing his word over mine, but from the way Ophelia's been hugging me and Rowan is gazing at me, not quite.

Rowan believes me. That's really sinking in now. He didn't like what I was telling him, but he took it to heart anyway.

"So if Soraya caught you," Indigo asks out of nowhere, "why didn't she just put you back with Gabriel?"

Like most little kids, she's always listening even when you think she's spacing out. "Who knows, Indigo? She doesn't talk. At least, not in a way I can understand. Rowan, can you tell what she's saying?"

He hesitates. "Soraya and I have our own language. We invented it together when we were small." Then Rowan seems to make up his mind about something. "I wasn't sure if we could trust you, Ada. Soraya's incredibly sensitive, and I was afraid of how hurt she'd be if you didn't react well when you saw her. And — you know, it would be way too dangerous for her if the normals ever found out she exists. But I'm actually relieved that you know all our secrets now, because it proves you're really part of the family." He says it a little too loudly, too decisively: it's not for me, it's for everyone listening.

All your secrets? Really, Rowan? I think.

But instead I say, "So can Marley know, too? I can see why you might be worried that Soraya would freak her out, but it seems weird not to tell her. Does she count as part of the family yet?"

I don't actually care that much about the answer. I'm mostly talking to cover the drumming of my heart as Gabe gets closer to the beach. But everyone except Rowan shoots nervous looks at one another.

"What?" I say. "Nothing happened to Marley, did it?"

"We weren't going to bring it up yet, Ada. Because you and Rowan went through a lot already today, and we thought . . . you don't need any more crazy news just now. Right?" Ophelia says. She pulls back and gives me a strange smile, like she's afraid I'll get mad.

Rowan stares. "Ophelia, tell us right now what's going on with Marley! Is she okay?"

"Um, she's okay. Don't worry. At least, she's not feeling too good right now. We've been trying to calm her down. But she *will* be okay. You know, in a while."

I scramble to my feet, ready to run up the hill. I can deal with Gabriel later. "Where is she?"

"Ada, it's really all right. Don't go, okay? She's in her room, and you can . . . At least, I think you'll be able to talk to her tomorrow. It's just that she's, um, she's building a chrysalis."

"What!"

"She's physically okay, really. Or she will be. But she's going through some heavy emotional drama because she wasn't expecting anything like this. Mr. Chu says it's not compatible with her self-image. Her instincts just took over, and she couldn't stop herself."

"A chrysalis?"

"So she's going to be a way bigger part of the family than she ever wanted to be," Rowan murmurs. If someone else had said that it might have seemed like gloating, but he sounds genuinely sad for her. "Poor Marley. She must be in complete shock."

I look out at the twilight-blue grass, the red-glowing bodies just above us now, the rising white blot of the mist-smeared moon. So is Marley going to be some kind of butterfly girl, or maybe a moth?

"Rowan!" Gabriel yells. He's glowing silvery white; there are moments when his skin lights up in a way that everyone can see. Bioluminescence is usually so beautiful, but on him it just gets on my nerves. Normally he'd jump dramatically off the grassy shelf, but he's limping pretty badly, and instead he sits down to slide onto the beach.

"Gabe!" Rowan gets up and runs to hug him. "Ada told me how you tried to grab her when she slipped into that pit in the cave. I guess you didn't see Soraya waiting there under the water? Anyway we're both fine. Soraya took care of Ada and got her back here safe. I can't remember anything that happened, so maybe she helped me out, too."

Gabriel turns to stare at me. He's trying to settle his skin, but blurts of magenta keep interrupting the silver glow. Ms. Stuart and maybe twenty of the kids are jumping and climbing down right behind him. He knows he can't say, *You told him what?*

"Don't feel bad, Gabe," I say loudly enough that everyone will hear. "You tried your hardest to reach me. I could hear you yelling for me as I was going down. And I really thought I was going to die when I hit the water, but then Soraya was right there and she caught me. I was terrified for a few seconds, but then she started sharing her air with me and I realized she was a friend."

I'm almost ready to laugh at the savage, bewildered look on his face. Then he gets a little bit more of a grip on himself.

"That was so great of Soraya, then. When I saw you go under, I was sure you weren't going to make it." His voice sounds so fake. Is he really fooling everyone?

"Right," I say. "So you had to go back and tell Ms. Stuart there was nothing you could do. That must have been awful."

"Ada!" Ms. Stuart says, walking across the sand. "And Rowan! I was afraid to believe it until I saw you both for myself. This could tempt me to adopt an irrational faith in miracles."

She hugs me. I don't hug her back, but she doesn't seem to notice.

"Ada, you seem to be covered in — what is it? Some kind of mucus?"

"Soraya's spit. She took my head inside her mouth so I could breathe."

Anywhere else people would flip out at that, but Ms. Stuart gives a wooden laugh. "Then a shower is in order. And both of you must be famished." I am, in fact.

She flashes Gabriel a hard-edged look and reaches for Rowan, who hugs her like he means it. "I can't imagine what we would have done if we'd lost you, Rowan. You're the living heart of this community." It's the first sincere thing anyone's said in a while.

We head back up the hill, and after we get cleaned up, Rowan and I sit in our pajamas with big bowls of spaghetti in our laps. They let us eat on the sofas in the lobby as a kind of reward for being alive, and after dinner there's a huge, flat chocolate cake that Mr. Chu baked in a hurry while we were showering. Rowan and I tell our lying stories over and over again, inventing new details when we have to. Everyone has so many questions. Indigo won't stop clinging to me, and Corbin is sprawled across Rowan's lap. It's after midnight, but nobody sends the small kids to bed, and they start drifting into sleep with their frosting-smudged noses in the carpet.

Rowan keeps beaming me warm, secretive smiles, and Gabriel sits cross-legged on the floor and watches me. I have to add a few parts to match the story he told while he thought

I was dead: *Oh, right, I did catch hold of a ledge inside that hole, and Gabriel was just throwing me the rope when my hand slipped. Totally. So much happened afterward that I forgot to mention that.*

I ask to see Marley, but they tell me she's asleep, or at least in some kind of trance, and that I shouldn't disturb her.

My head falls against the leather back of the sofa. I'm going to let my eyes close just for a moment. Just one, and then Ophelia and I will get our group of little kids ready for bed. We're being irresponsible, letting them stay up so late.

I'm dreaming about Indigo brushing her teeth when I half wake: just long enough to feel someone lowering me into my own bed.

When I found Rowan on the beach earlier, why was he crying? I really should have asked.

CHAPTER TWENTY-FOUR

"ADA! ADA! Ada!"

Marley's voice wakes me. She's screaming so loudly that no one anywhere near here will sleep through it. I jolt up and slide out of bed, fumbling my feet into my unlaced sneakers before I even understand what's happening. In the window the sky is lemon yellow with late dawn and the grass pitches like there might be a storm coming.

"Ada! Come! Melting words—almost dead—there's a message! Ada!"

I'm trying to make sense of what she's shouting as I dart through our door and into the hallway, Ophelia mumbling sleepy questions to my back.

Maybe there is no sense in it, though. Maybe whatever she's going through is making Marley delirious. Her room is at the back of the building around a bend, and she has it to herself—Gabriel never seemed to care about putting her with a roommate—but it's not nearly as nice as the others, some kind of converted linen closet with a cot and a dresser shoved into the corners. There are even shelves with stacks of white sheets going yellow from age, and dried-up bottles of cleaning supplies.

When I get there, the door is ajar. I push through and almost trip over Dr. Jacoway, who's sitting on the floor with his knees up and his chin propped on his folded arms. His body is so wide and full of folds that he looks like a crumpled tissue. He's staring rapturously at something over the dresser and doesn't react to me at all, even though I thumped into his back hard enough to bruise him.

That thing dangling over the dresser? It's made of what might be torn sheets, but they look weirdly shiny, stiff, brittle. They've been plastered into a lumpy shape like a huge peapod, glued to the ceiling somehow so that the lowest point twitches an inch above the dresser's scarred white top. Near the top there's a tuft of something coppery brown, curled and flicking rhythmically up and down.

Oh, no. That tuft is Marley's auburn curls.

All the rest of her has vanished inside that pod of matted sheets. Her chrysalis.

I don't think she can see me through the fabric, but she might sense me somehow because she starts screaming again. "Ada! Ada! I know! It came into my mind! A message in blue words, shining! Ada!"

Blue words? Really?

"Marley, I'm here. Everything's fine, you don't need to be

scared. I'm going to climb up on the dresser so we can talk, okay?"

"All night she writhed there as if she were encased in a dream, gorging up her wet lacquer onto the sheets, layering the bands about herself. She seemed to hear nothing, see nothing, beyond what was necessary for her task. Then with the dawn, she began to shudder, and then to scream," Dr. Jacoway murmurs, more to himself than to me. "An ordinary *sapiens* girl, so one might have thought, but revelation waited in her until the time was ripe. Most remarkable. Now she blossoms with surprise."

I wish he'd leave us alone, but from the way he's staring and smiling to himself, I'm pretty sure that's not happening. He's studying her as if she's the coolest thing he's ever seen.

I scramble up onto the dresser and carefully stand up, pressing against the wall. Marley's mostly still now, but sometimes she thrashes unpredictably and I'm afraid she'll knock me off. I want to look into the opening at the top of her chrysalis, to try and meet her eyes, but even on tiptoe I can't manage it, so I give up and wrap my arms around her shell of weirdly plasticky sheets. Even if she can't see me, it might comfort her a little to feel that I'm with her.

"I'm right here beside you, Marley. You can tell me anything you want, okay? You can whisper if you want. I'm right next to you." I can feel her shivering through the slick, awful material surrounding her. It bends slightly in a springy way.

"Ada?" Her voice is softer now, without the frenzied insanity.

"Yes, Marley."

"My mind was gone. Like dying. When I could think again, it was full of words."

Blue words. Maybe the blue truly communicated with her somehow? "What did it say?"

"That it's afraid for its children. It's afraid of what will happen to us. It says we're *hope* in terrible times that are coming, and we need to be protected from what she wants to do."

What Marley just said opens up so many crazy possibilities that I start wanting to believe she's out of her mind after all.

"It said that *we're* its children? Marley, that doesn't make any sense."

Or does it? The idea gives me a cold, queasy feeling. Was this what Rowan was trying to tell me yesterday?

I can feel her trembling violently inside her chrysalis. "It called us *daughters*. It called Gabriel *the violent child*. It said it won't help them, but they're very close now anyway, and it's afraid."

"Close to what?"

Marley doesn't answer that. Instead I hear the dry sound of a shredding cotton sheet and then a horrible noise. Marley must be coughing up something so thick and slimy that it nearly chokes her. Then, inside her shell, she starts to sob. Now even the gap that her hair stuck through is being pasted over. She's completely sealed in.

"Oh, Marley!" I wish I'd been a better friend to her. "You're going to be okay. You'll come out of there when it's time, and you'll be, you'll be amazing . . ."

"It won't be *me*, though." She barely gags out the words through her tears. "I won't see you again, Ada. I'm dissolving. Don't even call her Marley. Please? It won't be me."

"Marley!" She's making wet, gulping sounds in there, and I can't tell what's happening. "Dr. Jacoway! We need to stop this! We need to cut her out of there." Why didn't anyone think of that before?

"That would be the end of her, I'm afraid. From *this* death at least she can return to us transformed."

I don't know when I started crying. I'm stroking Marley's chrysalis, trying to soothe her while she jumps and gasps inside it.

"Seems like she's done talking for now," someone sneers from the doorway. "You won't be finding out that way, Ada."

I don't have to turn to know who it is. The door was open the whole time. Why didn't I stop to think who might be there listening?

Because I couldn't think, not about anything but Marley and everything she's going through. But I should have. I can't afford to let down my guard like that. Not ever.

"Poor Marley," I say without looking at him. "You heard her, didn't you? She said her mind is gone. Dissolving. No wonder everything she was saying was so totally disconnected from reality."

"The violent child? Me?" Gabriel says. I can hear the tight grin in his voice. It's like he thinks he just won some kind of point, though I don't know what the game is. "You're right, Ada. That's got nothing to do with anything."

I start to feel afraid that he might attack me again, even with Dr. Jacoway sitting there, and I turn and slide off the dresser. Marley's completely still now, and very quiet. I remember reading somewhere that caterpillars actually liquefy inside their chrysalises and then their bodies reassemble in their new shape. It makes sense if you think about it, since a butterfly doesn't look anything like a caterpillar with wings. How does it feel to let go of yourself so completely?

"Anyway, Ms. Stuart will be glad to hear we're close. She was worried we were on the wrong track; like, that she might need to start over from scratch. I can tell her we don't need your floating blue whatever after all. And that means we don't need you, either. See, I've been *telling* her we should just lock you up until you fold, but now — I don't know, feeding a prisoner sounds like a waste of our resources."

I can't stand looking at him anymore. He's handsome, sure, but in such a cold way that it's worse than any ugliness. His skin has that flat whiteness it gets when he's feeling especially self-satisfied. I decide to ignore his threats; that's not the part that really matters.

"You mean, you're getting close with that project you were telling me about? *In the cave?* That's great, Gabriel. But close to what?"

"Like you don't know!" Gabriel snaps. "Like I wasn't right there in the room when you were jabbering on about your *theory* to Dr. Jacoway here. You didn't figure that much out by yourself, either. I don't know what you were trying to do, saying all that garbage right in my face. But it didn't work, Ada."

"Her theory?" Dr. Jacoway asks. "But this can't be the same girl—the one who spoke of Aphrodite, who claimed that she had risen from the waves in just the same manner. Or is there some resemblance, after all?"

I don't say anything. Gabriel thinks I know a lot more than I really do, that's obvious. And whatever they're up to, it seems like it must have something to do with the algae I was talking about: algae that can carry entire chromosomes among different species. I think of those petri dishes in Ms. Stuart's office with their glaze of reddish dust. Of course: red algae are the kind that can write over sections of DNA.

Gabriel said there was some problem stopping them. He said the blue could solve it, or at least they *believe* that's true. Does that problem have something to do with the fact that Chimera Syndrome occurs only on Long Island? Because if I know anything about Gabriel, he'd absolutely love to see chimeras spread all over the world. That's the war he's always dreaming about, a conquest: more and more and more of us, until we take over. And if I was right about the algae, why *hasn't* the syndrome spread by now? Is there something keeping it contained?

The blue is afraid for its children, Marley said. Its *daughters.* That includes her and me, Ophelia and Soraya and Indigo.

No wonder Dr. Jacoway doesn't remember the scientists at Novasphere working on the algae that brought chimeras into being. People massacred those scientists for no reason at all.

I see it now. Something *else* changed the algae, reengineered it as a way to create us. Something with powers we don't understand: a shining tangle of blue brilliance that nurtures part-human tadpoles in the dark, that calls us *darling*.

Those poor scientists. They had nothing to do with it.

CHAPTER TWENTY-FIVE

I'M SUPPOSED to go to class. I'm supposed to sit at that conference table across from Gabriel, and act calm, and read *The Tempest* aloud with everyone, wondering the whole time what Gabe is planning for me now that he's completely sure they don't need me—to act as an interpreter between them and the blue, to coax it into helping them with their war on the normals. If the blue could create us here, it could do the same thing everywhere, or at least everywhere near the ocean; that must be their reasoning. As I get dressed and head down the hallway to breakfast, I'm thinking about what today will be like and wondering how I'll stand it.

"Ada? You saw Marley, right? Is she okay?" It's Ophelia, fluttering up behind me.

"Not really. It's like she's losing herself. It's not quite as bad as dying, but I think for her it feels pretty close to that." The hall is jostling with kids. I catch a glimpse of Gabriel's hand blinking blue and orange between the clustered bodies ahead of us, and my mind's not really on the conversation.

"But—she's going to have wings! She might be able to fly! Did you point that out to her, Ada? How phenomenal it's going to be? Because I think you might be the only person here she'll really listen to." I can feel the cool stir of wind as Ophelia hover-hops along. The ceiling isn't high enough here for her to launch herself upward, and I get the feeling that she hates it more every time her toes touch down on the carpet.

"I did tell her that. But she says that whatever she turns into, it won't be her anymore. Not—not her *real* self."

She flurries around me and turns, softly curling a hand on my shoulder. "Ada? You seem sad. I know you're worried about Marley, but that's not all that's wrong, is it?"

I think about how to answer. Gabriel might tell her part of what Marley said; he'll give her a version of it that's useful for him, anyway. "She was saying some crazy things. Like— whatever accident happened to make the chimeras, whether it was the scientists at Novasphere or whatever—Marley was calling us its daughters. And I guess that made me miss my real parents."

Ophelia nods. She's walking close to me now with one wing brushing my shoulder blades. "Have you heard anything from them?"

It's a sensitive subject for everyone here, so I usually avoid it. But Ophelia sounds like she really cares about the answer, and maybe I can admit this much. "I've been too scared to check my email. I know I should, but I just can't make myself do it."

"Would it help if I stayed with you while you checked? You know, for moral support?" The shimmer on her eyes almost swirls; maybe she's feeling anxious about something herself.

I smile at her. It took me a while, but now the complicated green-black sparkle of her compound eyes doesn't seem alien or eerie to me at all. They're beautiful, and they're so right for her. "Thanks. I think that might make it easier."

Personally, I'd way rather believe we were all a disastrous mistake, the result of some experiment gone horribly awry at Novasphere, than accept my new idea: that the blue truly is our parent, that it made us for reasons of its own. But maybe that's because I have real parents out there, and I don't like the idea of them being replaced by some floating inhuman thing, even if it is beautiful. Just thinking about it makes my insides twist, and I want to escape from ever having that thought again.

Rowan and Ophelia might feel differently, though. They might go crazy with longing at the realization that they have a parent who never abandoned them, who drifted and nestled around them in their sleep, even if they could never see it. I can imagine that would feel like a huge improvement over the way their human parents acted, sending them away as soon as they were born. As soon as they saw how their babies stirred their shining wings, curled their flippers.

Maybe that's why Rowan was crying. Maybe that's why he was ready to lie to Gabe and Ms. Stuart. If he thinks he's found a parent who actually loves him, he'll probably do almost anything it wants.

In the dining room Ophelia catches my hand to tow me over to the table where Gabriel and Rowan are already sitting, both of them staring at me, though in very different ways. I pull away from her. "I hope you don't mind. I need a little time alone right now. Seeing Marley like that really upset me."

She gives me a little hug. "Don't worry, Ada. And I bet Marley's going to absolutely adore her brand-new self when she hatches, even if she doesn't think so now. You should be happy for her! But I understand. We won't be hurt if you want to sit by yourself today."

I head for the table where Marley huddled on her own our first night here. Breakfast is oatmeal with brown sugar and raisins and an apple on the side. I stir the oatmeal and swallow a few bites, but it's hard to feel hungry. Gabriel and Rowan go on looking over at me to the point where it's embarrassing, and Ophelia leans in close to Gabe. They keep whispering into each other's ears, and I know I've made another mistake by not sitting with them, because now I can't stop wondering what they're talking about.

I watch while Gabe slides his arm around her shoulders, just above the place where her wings jut out. He's never done that before, I'm certain. I watch her blush. But he's smiling at me while he holds her. I have to remind myself that Ophelia has no idea what he did to me — that I lied to her about it myself—so of course she doesn't think of cuddling up to him as a betrayal. But it still hurts. She must at least realize how much he hates me.

Is he just using her as a way to hurt me? If he is, that's so sick I'd like to smash his sprained ankle with a hammer.

Way before everyone else is done eating, I clear my place and walk out. I weave through the corridors and find a torn vinyl chair in a dark corner of the library. I feel cold and nauseous, and I stare at the screens of those two old computers as if my parents' voices might start bubbling out of them, telling me they miss me, telling me they never should have let me go. But I still can't make myself turn one on.

It's time for class. I never cut classes at my old school, and I know I shouldn't try it here. Everyone will notice. They might even send somebody to search for me. But suddenly I don't care.

Maybe my parents don't want me, but I still have a sister. She's strong and wild and fierce, bashing her way through the ocean, not hanging around here for everyone to treat her like she's some kind of enemy. Soraya goes where she wants, and she doesn't follow anyone's rules.

And if she and Rowan invented their own language, then maybe the two of us can learn to communicate, too. She's got to be just as lonely as I am.

I stay where I am while the hallway outside turns into a river of laughing, cooing, shrieking voices. The shadows are deep, and a maze of bookcases fills the space, so probably no one will notice me through the glass door. The vinyl chair slurps at my bare shoulders and sweat pools under my thighs, but I don't move, and eventually the voices drain away. Maybe Ophelia will tell everyone I'm so agitated over Marley that they'll decide to let me have some time to myself. Maybe no one will bother me.

When it's been quiet for a few minutes, I slip to a spot where I can peer above a row of books — the bookcases are the cheap kind made of riveted metal with no backs to them — and then through the door. Gray shadows cling to the scarred, graffitied paint, and the lights buzz in the emptiness. There are rooms used for classes along this hallway, including our conference room, so I slide out of the library and walk along fast with my head bowed, heading back to my bedroom. I need to get something. I need Soraya to hear me, to know how much I care about reaching her.

Five minutes later, I'm running through the parched golden grass with my violin case thudding against my thigh.

CHAPTER TWENTY-SIX

I

T'S A hot day, but the air feels muggy and closed in. The sky is sunless and covered in fuzzy dots of cloud like gray mold. In the dimness between the clouds, shapes like lilac feathers spin. I wish there were a cliff to stand on, even a low one, but there isn't, and the grassy shelf seems too far back from the water. The last thing I want Soraya to think is that I'm trying to keep my distance so she can't touch me. After scanning the waves for a few moments, I decide to walk right to the sand's edge, but not into the water. It's high tide so I don't have to walk far.

The sea is exceptionally rough today, the waves huge. The wind isn't that strong, but it has a strange, stifled feeling, as if there were something it felt too shy to say.

Like me. Now that I'm here, I wonder what right I have to bother her. I'm taking it for granted that she's horribly lonely, and that she needs me as much as I need her, but Ophelia said that Soraya likes being on her own. Just because she didn't let me die, I can't assume she wants anything to do with me.

I take my time tightening the bow and stroking on the rosin, and while I do, I'm wondering if she's watching me. From what Rowan said, I know she saw my face before I ever saw hers, maybe the first time I was playing in the water with Ophelia. She could have been hiding under the surface on the far side of the fence the whole time, looking in at me with the same weird recognition I felt when I saw her. Maybe she even slipped through the hole to watch me. Since she's cold-blooded, it wouldn't necessarily be easy for me to spot her.

Thunder screams and then grumbles away to nothing. I don't have time to spend being indecisive. The waves arch up, steely and dark, then burst on the sand and fan almost to my feet. Knife-thin pink glints twirl through the receding water, and I remember my dad saying, *No, no. The sea is only blue or green or gray, except at sunset. This isn't sunset, Ada.*

I lift the violin to my shoulder and let a high, slow note vibrate out across the air. A call. Will she understand?

Again. I play longer, deeper, seesawing notes, trying to imitate the groaning cries she made when she was searching for Rowan. If they have a language together, then I'll try to speak it. *Say it with music, Ada. Never words. Music is safe.*

Meanwhile my own voice keeps rising in my throat, making a sound somewhere between laughing and stifled crying. I don't think my dad would call it *safe* to try and summon a giant human-squid hybrid, even one who shares my face, out of the sea. My eyes fill with tears, and the sparks of pink light on the waves spread out into blurry, cherry-laced stars. How can I miss someone I don't even know, someone who can't speak a single word to me?

My sister, I try to play. *My twin. We were ripped apart before we were ever born, but we've found each other now. I'm land and you're sea, but we can look into each other and see ourselves for the first time. Chimera, chimirror. Please come, Soraya, I'm waiting.*

Lightning breaks the sky like a teacup. If it starts to rain, I'll have to give up — I can't let my violin get wet — but right now I can't make myself stop. So much has happened, and I haven't let myself really feel any of it, because if I do it will be too much, too overwhelming. But I can let it sing and clang out from the instrument vibrating against my chin. I can try to explain it all to *her.*

My eyes drift closed. I see ruby lights shimmered over with dancing flecks of icy green.

A raindrop pocks my cheek. *I have to stop, to stop, to stop,* I play, but I can't pull myself out of the music I'm making. I guess to most people it would sound horrible, a yowl, a shredded-metal cry. But it's the truth. Marley is dissolving into juice and Gabriel wants me dead and there's a really dangerous plot going on, and maybe even the people here I care about most are in on it. If I try to stop them — though how can I stop them? — then possibly even Ophelia and Rowan will turn against me. I can't be sure of anything, and there's no softness in that. No harmony.

But there is a kind of beauty in it, just like Dr. Jacoway said.

Another drop thuds down, right on the fingerboard this time. I force my eyes open. I have to pick up the case where I left it on the sand, put the violin away, shut the clasps.

A dark swell is slicing through the water in front of me. It's inside the fence and moving at fantastic speed, tiny lacy wavelets pouring along its flanks like long hair feathered back by the wind.

I have just time to gasp before Soraya wraps a tentacle around my waist and swings me up into the sky. It's so sudden that my bow slips from my hand. She catches it delicately in a single sucker and passes it back to me, and I take it before I have time to feel surprised.

It's incredible how strong she is. One tentacle is enough to keep me swaying in midair, sea foam snaking away below me as the waves crest and smash. She gazes up at me, her huge gray face tipped back as if the water were a pillow, her green-gold eyes sad and serious. How can I see myself in a being so different from anything I've ever known? But I do.

I didn't notice last time, but Soraya has two shorter, thinner tentacles in addition to her twisting mass of long arms. The short ones end in enormous, slippery-looking gray hands the size of the seats on the cafeteria's chairs. She reaches up with one hand now and strokes my cheek. Because I've been crying. She's brushing away a tear.

Maybe she hated me before, but she doesn't now.

"Soraya!" I say. "You knew, you understood me. I'm so happy."

She puts one of her human-shaped fingers to my lips — just the tip is enough to cover half my face — and then moves it to touch the violin. Of course she doesn't want me to use words, not when she can't. It's not fair.

I know I shouldn't be playing my violin out in the rain. If it gets ruined, I'll have no way to replace it, and then I'll be even lonelier here, and even more voiceless, than I am already.

But this is more important.

I play for my sister: fragments of Stravinsky's concerto in D mixed in with whirls of improvisation, long tonal cries. And as I play I'm racing through the air, dipping and weaving in her grasp, with my long hair tangling in my face and gusts full of raindrops striking me at odd angles. She's zooming me around like a four-year-old would a toy airplane. Sometimes my eyes are full of violet-ringed storm clouds, sometimes dashing waves. Sometimes Soraya moans beneath me, speaking to me in a language I can only understand if I completely forget about words. I'm breathless with laughter and giddiness, flying over the sea.

Then I feel something soft churning at my feet, and look down to see my shoes skimming through the sand. Soraya lets me go, and I stumble onto my knees, too dizzy to keep my balance. My violin jolts from my grip, but luckily it lands softly. I lean forward with my head still spinning to pick it up.

Soraya bellows and I hear a warning sharpness in her tone. Ms. Stuart is standing on the bluff watching us, and Soraya is already thirty yards back from the shore, only her eyes peering above the water. I understand at once: she doesn't want Ms. Stuart to see her face. She doesn't want her to know what we are to each other.

It's private.

"Ada," Ms. Stuart says dryly. "That was an impressive performance. From both of you. It's unfortunate that I was your only audience."

"I wasn't performing. I was trying to communicate."

"And what were you trying to say?"

That's too complicated to answer, even if it were any of her business. "Soraya saved my life. I wanted to say thank you." I scramble to my feet, pick up my case, and shake the sand out before I settle the violin back in its hollow and tuck the bow into its groove in the lid. I snap the case shut without looking at her. I wish my cheeks weren't getting hot, that my stomach wasn't tight with anger. My meeting with Soraya was so magical and so secret that I hate the thought of anyone watching us, especially *her*.

When I glance back at the water, Soraya's already gone. A circle of foam, already fragmenting with the surge, shows where she dove to slip through the hole in the fence. Why couldn't she just take me with her?

Probably because she knows as well as I do that I have nowhere else to go.

"You've made your point, then. And since attending class wasn't worth your time today, perhaps now you'd be willing to walk with me?"

I think about that. "Where would we go?"

"Why not show me where you went when you chose to go adventuring in the dead of night? I heard you sustained some damage from the blackberry thickets." She nods at my calf. I hadn't noticed, but one leg of my jeans is shoved up, damp with sea spray. My exposed skin is striped with the dark scabs I got while I was running away from the blue.

"I didn't go anywhere special. Just to the edge of the woods." I feel a little sick, though, at the realization that Ophelia must have reported on me. She's the one who saw me go to bed the other night with unmarked legs and wake up covered in scratches. Every time I start thinking I can really trust her, something happens to rip that trust away from me.

Rowan said that Ophelia is on my side *as much as she can be.* I guess *as much as she can be* just isn't much at all.

"To the edge of the woods, then. I have something I'd like to say to you. I think a misunderstanding has come between us, Ada, and I'd like to clear it up if I can."

I don't think it's a misunderstanding, I almost say, but then I decide it's smarter to keep my mouth shut. And maybe this way I'll learn something. "Okay." I shove my case up onto the grassy shelf and climb after it. The rain seems like it's backing off for now, though the clouds are dark and pushing along in huge blue currents.

"Do you know what we mean, Ada, when we talk about someone internalizing the prejudice against them?"

That takes me a moment. I pick up the case and hold it tight against my chest. I miss my sister already; why did Ms. Stuart have to come here and interrupt us? "It means

—taking it in. Believing that you're not worth very much just because other people tell you so."

"And how would you respond if I said that you've internalized society's irrational fear of the chimeras? That you've *taken in* their idea that what you are makes you somehow less worthy? Less deserving of freedom?"

I don't want to listen to this, but my cheeks flush with the suspicion that she might be right—at least a little bit right. "It's not that I think we're not worth as much! I just think we might be dangerous—and until they really know for sure that it's safe to let us out—I mean, I understand why we have to be here. Everybody outside has a good reason to be afraid of us."

Though, realistically, Soraya is free. That must be the true reason they didn't want me to know about her. And there could be hundreds of other kimes out there, for all I know: mostly animal ones that aren't supposed to exist and that nobody has really noticed yet. Spiders with tiny human mouths could be lurking in people's woodpiles; crows with human eyes could be watching people's parking lots. Probably Rowan is right, and we're just locked up to make everybody feel better.

"Yes, that's what they've told you. Again and again. You've taken in their message about the threat you supposedly represent—the end of humanity, no less. You've made that message part of yourself, and now you stand here and repeat it. This is precisely the internalization I was referring to. I began my career as a lab assistant for Dr. Jacoway, before he worked at Novasphere; did you know that? I was entirely devoted to the ideals of science. When he first came here, he asked me to join him, and because I admired him so much I accepted. Being some combination of foster mother and prisoner was nothing at all like the life that I imagined for myself when I was young, but then—I came to care. I'm sure that most people would say I care too much. Ada, no one alive is more committed to the rights of children like you than I am. No one has worked harder on your behalf."

"I know that." But the blue doesn't trust her, and I don't, either.

"If you struggle against me, then you are also struggling against yourself. Against your own future. You see why I might find this cause for concern."

I hesitate. "I know you want to help us. You'd probably fight to the death for us. I *know* that."

"But?"

"But I think you might be fighting in the wrong way."

We haven't even made it to the edge of the woods, just strayed a short distance over the grass. Now we've stopped dead to stare at each other. The grass is an eerily bright mustard-gold under the moody purplish gray of the clouds.

"I suppose you know exactly what way that is? You've pursued your investigations, come to your own conclusions?"

There's something horrible in her face now, but I don't know what it is. If I'm right about what she and Gabriel are plotting, then it seems obvious regular humans would retaliate. Does she really think they'd let us get away with it? "Not really. I know you're trying something."

A pause. "And can you try to understand how utterly frustrating it is to raise children, all the while knowing that they'll be thwarted from fulfilling their true potential? Of course I want to change the situation."

When she says it like that, I almost start to wonder if she's right and I'm the one making a mistake. Almost. "But what if trying to change it just makes everything worse?"

"You know, Ada, I've had another thought about you. I was reluctant to entertain it seriously, though, since it would imply that you're the pawn of some extremely unscrupulous people. There might be a simpler explanation for your behavior than ordinary self-loathing."

"Like what?"

"Your father. Isn't he Dr. Caleb Lahey?"

CHAPTER TWENTY-SEVEN

Y ES," I SAY. "He is. But I don't see—"

"It's time you returned to class, Ada. I have work to do. As always."

Her cropped hair is so thin that the wind opens up big pink zigzags of scalp. I can smell her sweat, and there are dark stains on her grayish dress, like maybe she spilled a cup of coffee on herself and never had time to change.

"I really don't understand what you were saying. I don't see what my dad has to do with anything."

"Of course you don't. Get back to class. I understand that you're not overly fond of Gabriel, but avoiding him isn't an option. Personal irritations of that kind can't be allowed to interfere with the functioning of our community."

I can't tell her that attempted murder doesn't count as an *irritation.* And anyway I'm too distracted by what she said about my dad. My heart is smacking in my chest, and I'm close to crying from fury.

"Are you calling my dad unscrupulous? He's not. And he only let me come here because my mom was so worried about their new baby. That I would infect it."

Weirdly, she smiles at that. Slyly. "That's quite a burden for them to put on you, Ada. At least one of your parents is almost certainly a carrier of Chimera Syndrome already. It generally attacks the germ cells in the mother at the same time as the embryo, if a woman happens to be pregnant—or possibly your father's sperm cells were infected before you were ever conceived. And since he's a microbiologist, he must be well aware that their new baby is at risk in any case. There's no good reason to believe that you're contagious at all, in reality. The menace of the chimeras is simply a myth cherished by the ignorant. It's interesting, isn't it, that the authorities haven't tried to disillusion them?"

"That can't be true." That's the only reason why he didn't fight harder for me: that having me around might actually kill my new sibling. I understood why I had to go. I *understood.*

"Go to class. If you decide later that you have more to discuss with me, I promise to find time for you."

That's it: this is all a trick. Gabriel said that I'm holding out on them because of my parents. If he believes that, then Ms. Stuart probably does too. She's lying to make me hate my dad. To make me rely on her and tell her everything, everything I've seen and felt and thought here, and then sign up to help her with her *project.* But I won't be discussing anything with her.

I turn away and storm back up the hill without another

word. As I reach the front door, the sky splits with light and thunder shrieks behind me. Rain slams down at my heels, and I pause in the lobby, feeling off balance and breathless, while the roof drums fiercely overhead.

I'm not about to go to class, though. Not when I can't stop crying. I turn and run through the halls, trying to reach my bedroom before anyone sees me like this. And all at once the blue is around me, wrapping my face and billowing back from my hands. I see the hallway in front of me warped and electric, bluer than the sky and darting with violet shapes like minnows. When I reach my room and fall onto the bed, it bundles itself around my shoulders, charging me as if the storm were against my skin, and brushes the insides of my eyes.

It's trying to comfort me, and I guess I appreciate it. I wish I could ask it what I should do.

I wish it could tell me that Ms. Stuart was absolutely lying. That there wasn't a speck of truth in anything she said. My father would never deceive me that way. If it weren't for their new baby, he would have fought for me. He would have faced down the mobs if they threatened us and kept me safe at home, just like he said to Mr. Collins the day they took me away.

In fact, if there was any truth at all in what Ms. Stuart told me, then that would mean every single thing my father said to me and Mr. Collins that day was an act. There's no reason why he would do that.

In the next moment I'm back on my feet, wiping my face. I'm nauseous and my knees are wobbling, but I have to get to the library. There must be an email from him—I'm sure of it. One that will explain everything. It's only a little after noon, so no one will be in there.

The blue strokes my face, then pours through the wall and over the meadow. I can see a faint azure ruffling in the grass as it slides away. And the funny thing is that I do feel a little stronger, knowing that it cares about me. Whatever it is, and whatever it wants from us. It could have made us for completely selfish reasons, or by accident, or just as some kind of chaotic game, but it still came to me when I was crying and held me.

And if my dad really did betray me, the blue might turn out to be the only parent I have left. Then I'll need it just as much as Rowan does.

I slip back down the hall as quickly and softly as I can. The air seems to pulse with the beat of the rain overhead, and my heart patters in my chest. Whatever might be lurking in my inbox feels like an even bigger, darker, wilder threat than Soraya seemed to be when she was still hiding at the bottom of the pit.

Now and then voices drift around corners and I freeze against the marker-scrawled walls, but no one comes, and no one notices me, and a few minutes later, I'm tugging back the library's glass door and slipping up to the computers. They're at a table where anyone walking by will be able to see me. I'll try to be fast.

All at once I realize that I'm acting as if there really will be messages from my dad that no one here should see. Messages that might put me in danger. It's like I believe everything Ms. Stuart said and, even worse, everything she didn't quite come out and say. But how can I?

I reach to power up the computer on the right, standing next to its drab school chair. I'm full of a jerky energy, and I can't make myself sit. The machine hesitates, then gasps out a sleepy wheezing. The screen flashes from dead gray to deep blue, and the computer gives out another sound halfway between a sigh and a grind, and then just stops doing anything.

It's chilly in here. It takes me a moment to realize that the tall, skinny windows all along the back wall have been left open, and the rain is driving through and spattering on the books. It seems irresponsible not to go and close them all. A gust full of droplets prickles my arm, but I'm not about to step away from the computer.

It takes all my willpower not to smack the blue screen. There's another grunt, like the computer might decide to do something someday, and then a cursor appears and blinks at me. I grab the mouse and shove it back and forth. Nothing.

Seconds lurch by. I keep twisting to look over my shoulder, sure that someone is watching me through the door, but the hallway stays as blank and gray as ever, and finally, finally a handful of icons winks onto the screen, including one for a search engine. I double click, and an hourglass appears.

This time I'm sure: there are voices out in the hall. But they're still too far away for me to see their glow. I should be able to see them coming before they see me, at least if I keep peering back that way.

The rain is so loud, though. I'll never hear footsteps. Not if someone is trying to be sneaky.

I finally get to the page for my email and sign in with my hands trembling.

My inbox opens. There are dozens of messages, from Nina and Harper and other kids I'm not even really friends with, Olivia and Luke and Simonetta. I open the first one. *Ada I just want you to know that NO ONE believes what they're saying about you! NO ONE! You can come back and we will laugh at anybody who calls you the k-word. K?*

But most of them are from my dad. The other messages from my friends can wait.

Ada, dearest, by now you must have found my letter and the new phone. I'm afraid you're upset with me now that you see how I've planned for this moment, and that's why you haven't written. I don't want you to put yourself at risk in any way. Just be quietly observant, as you always are.

That's from the day after I arrived.

Right; I never opened my duffle. I didn't want to know.

Maybe this is exactly what I didn't want to find out.

Something with sharp metal wings seems to be crashing around inside my forehead, trying to get out. My vision blurs for a moment, and I can't keep reading. Then I refocus and start clicking on his messages at random, reading a sentence or two and then jumping to the next. I should shut off the computer and dart away before those voices in the hallway come any closer, before someone catches me here, but I'm not ready to tear my eyes from the screen. Because what I'm thinking can't be true. It *can't.*

Ada, I'm getting worried. You did destroy my letter immediately, as I asked? It could be open to interpretation . . .

You did not choose to be what you are. There should be no need for you to redeem yourself for something you can't help. I know that. But unfortunately there is. This is your chance to help all of humanity and to prove that you are truly a part of humankind. Get the information they want, and our family will be given special permission to leave Long Island. You won't have to register.

At least write. No matter how angry you are, we don't deserve this silence from you! Or are they preventing you somehow?

I never wanted it to be you, Ada. But your eyesight . . . I knew that our best chance of discovering . . .

If I come it will only cast suspicion on you. I'm afraid to take the risk.

That was yesterday evening. That was when I was whipping through the ocean with my head in Soraya's mouth, breathing her breath.

Ms. Stuart was right. My dad sent me here to be a spy. After all his talk about keeping me safe, he was fine with sending me into danger when it seemed like I might be useful. Does he really think I would prove I'm good enough to be part of *humanity* by betraying my own kind? My friends, my own sister? That's what he thinks is supposed to redeem me?

I think I've been forgetting to breathe. When I try to stand up, darkness rushes through me and I sink back down. Maybe I pass out for a few moments, maybe longer, because the next thing I know, my head is on the keyboard, full of stabbing pain.

When I look around, I see a trail of softly luminous red warmth in the air beside me, already fading out. Within the last few seconds, someone was standing over my shoulder, reading the message that's up on the screen now, even though I never clicked on it. I see the words through a blur.

I'm coming, Ada. It's time to get you out.

That was sent today.

CHAPTER TWENTY-EIGHT

I TRY TO STAND, to run out into the hall before who-ever was reading my email has time to vanish, but I must be getting sick. The shelves rock like boats, and darkness keeps waving in my eyes.

There's a searing pain on the side of my neck. I start to understand: somebody did something to me. I touch the spot and feel a rising welt, like a burn. I find myself clutching the handle on the library door to keep myself upright, and then I see it on the gray carpet: a thin pink worm, phasing in and out of focus. One of the short, poisonous tentacles from Indigo's stomach—somebody took it and used it as a weapon. From what Ophelia told me, I'll be unconscious very soon.

I expect the door to be locked, but then the handle turns and I'm through, standing unsteadily in the hallway. It feels like the floor has melted beneath me.

I see the red glow driving at me in the dimness, but I'm too weak to get away. There are at least three of them coming up behind me, yanking my arms back. I feel rough hands pinning my wrists together. I think I might fall.

"I didn't do anything," I say. It comes out slurred. "I didn't even know what he wanted. Not until right now."

"Of course I was concerned once I realized whose daughter she was. I simply couldn't bring myself to accept that anyone would exploit his own child that way. It's barbaric." That's Ms. Stuart's voice, but she's not talking to me. "Ophelia is searching their room."

"He's coming here," Gabriel says. "That's what the last message said. It was sent an hour ago, so he could be here anytime."

"Then prepare yourself. You know what you have to say."

What's that supposed to mean? I try to ask. I don't hear my voice at all anymore.

"What if he doesn't believe me?"

"In all probability, he won't. No one doubts Dr. Lahey's intelligence. Tell him anyway, and be ready to repeat the story as often as necessary. You'll have to talk to the police as well."

"Where's Rowan? He won't want to believe this."

"I'm well aware of that. I'll have him read the emails for himself. And the letter, assuming Ophelia finds it."

I'm being hustled along the hall now, or maybe carried. I don't think I feel the floor. *Rowan,* I try to say, *I didn't do it! I wouldn't spy on you!* But then I realize vaguely that he's not even here.

They drop me in a windowless room a lot like the supply closet that Marley's been using as a bedroom. I hear the door lock behind me. My legs slide out from under me, and I find myself sitting on the floor with my back to the wall, staring at the brown lines crossing through the yellow linoleum.

Do I pass out? That's probably what it would look like, but to me it feels like I just disappear.

* * *

"You can't just lock her up! You can't! There's no proof she even did anything!" Rowan is screaming his head off. He sounds so desperate that my heart reaches for him through the wall. The doorknob rattles like he just grabbed for it, and then there's a scuffling sound as someone pulls him back. In the crack under the door I can just see the slight red cast by his warmth. *His* warmth. *Rowan.*

I almost scream for him, but I have the sense to stop myself in time. It's more important to listen. It's way better if they think I'm still unconscious. How long has it been?

"Rowan, Rowan, Rowan. Listen to me. There's no choice. Ada knows everything. She knows about the algae. She knows we've been trying to reengineer it so it doesn't die as soon as it leaves the coastal waters right around Long Island. If only Dr. Jacoway still had his old brilliance, we'd be so much further, but . . . I admire Ada's character as much as you do, Rowan. She's a brave girl. But she's working against us, and we cannot allow her to ruin our efforts. I need you to accept that." It's Ms. Stuart. Will he believe her?

"She wouldn't do that. She cares too much—about us."

"Rowan, think about it. Ada had arranged to check her email with Ophelia beside her. For moral support, supposedly. Clearly she was rushing to delete all the incriminating emails before that could happen, so Ophelia would only see the un-opened messages from her old friends. What more proof do we need?"

It sounds like Rowan is crying, but in a muffled way, so maybe she's holding him. He'll have her coarse dress against his fur, the stink of her sweat in his nose.

"She's been coming out and *saying*—all kinds of things, that she thinks kimes are a big threat and that people are right to be scared of us. She told Ophelia she'd feel terrible if her parents' new baby was one of us. She knew how much it both-ered us, too, when she kept saying stuff like that. If Ada were spying, she would have told us whatever we wanted to hear."

Rowan's still standing up for me, but he's not screaming anymore. He's starting to break down instead, and his voice is getting weaker. Ms. Stuart is winning.

"Oh—I'm sure that once Ada got to know everyone here, she felt deeply guilty about what her father had asked her to do. I don't think she lacks heart, Rowan. She's been say-ing more than she should in an effort to justify herself. To talk herself into betraying all of us. It's truly appalling that her fa-ther put her in this position, where she was bound to be torn by conflicting loyalties."

"You told him Ada is *dead*. You and Gabriel—it's hor-rible."

"Frankly, Rowan, I think he deserves to live with the

consequences of his actions. He should have thought about that before he sent his twelve-year-old daughter in here as a spy."

Dead. What did I expect them to tell him? I bet they used Gabriel's old story about that underground crevice. They probably said I fell into the dark and there was no way to reach my body.

And if he believes them, then no one will ever come to get me out of here.

"Let her out. I'll watch her. I'll make sure she doesn't cause any problems, Ms. Stuart. I promise."

"No. Rowan, I never thought I would say this, but I don't entirely trust you. Not where Ada is concerned."

I still feel sick and bleary; the toxins from little Indigo's tentacle must be pretty strong. Everything they're saying beats at my brain, and I struggle to understand it. So parasitic algae do cause Chimera Syndrome, okay — I basically knew that. But didn't Ms. Stuart just say that the algae can't live in the water away from Long Island? Why wouldn't they live just as well anywhere?

I drift off again, and all I see is moving blue: blue clouds and blue cascades, numbers and staircases and brilliant cobalt chandeliers. The blue must be with me, hugging my eyes as I slide in and out of sleep. And *blue words,* bright and so delicate they'll shatter if I try to catch hold of them: something about a world that might be breaking. Something about new life in new shapes flowering in the ruins, blue running through our veins like luminous sap, charging us, making us stretch and grow. *Us,* the chimeras. Is that why the blue made us? *Life is glowing,* I try to say, but my voice seems far away from me. *Life is what glows when you think it's all gone dark.*

At one point I wake up and find dinner next to me: roast chicken and little buttered potatoes and chocolate chip cookies. A big glass of milk. It's fancier than the food we usually get; maybe somebody out there feels bad about how they're treating me. I manage to sit up on a crate, though my head still feels wobbly, and start to eat with the dish perched on my knees. It's barely warm. I have no idea how long I've been in here. A loud metal clanging sounds in the distance; for a long, confused moment, I think it might be some bizarre clock, chiming the hours. Whatever it is, I think I've heard it before.

"Hello?" I call, raising my voice to be heard over the clashing sound. It rakes, bangs, squeals. Why won't it stop? "Hello? Is anyone there?"

No reply. I get off the crate and kneel down to peer through the crack below the door. The hallway is dimly lit, and there's no haze of red warmth for as far as I can see, in any direction. Apart from the distant ruckus, it seems weirdly silent.

"Hello?"

My brain is just starting to work again, because all at once I recognize what that noise is: the mob is back, and from the ferocity of the slamming, they must be making a serious effort to break down the gate. Has everyone run away? Did they completely forget about me? I picture the hotel burning, everybody running for the woods or the sea, with me still locked in this room and Marley, poor Marley, helplessly dangling in her chrysalis.

Adrenaline floods through me, and I stand up and beat on the door. "Hey, I'm still trapped in here! Where is everyone? Please, somebody, answer me!"

In a lull between slams, I think I hear something near the door, but it's so soft I can't be sure. A whispery noise, like a hand brushing wood.

"Hello? Is someone there?"

No answer, so I drop to the floor again and twist my neck to peek through the crack. I don't see even a hint of red warmth.

But I do see two objects moving, shifting gently and restlessly from side to side on the hallway carpet. After staring in bewilderment, I realize what they are. They're only inches from my face.

A pair of damp bare feet the color of pale jade.

CHAPTER TWENTY-NINE

THOSE FEET are big enough to belong to a grown man, or even bigger — it's definitely not anyone I know here. Maybe I made a huge mistake by yelling and calling attention to myself. The feet step back, the shadows move, and then a greenish finger slithers under the door and brushes my forehead; it's cold, amphibious, sticky. I pull away with a cry and jump to my feet.

There's a quiet slurping noise. An instant later, I get it: that thing is sucking the taste of my skin off its finger. My heart skips at a broken rhythm, and I stumble backwards, pressing against the far wall. The crashing at the gate has started again, and now there are staticky voices booming through loudspeakers as well, too warped for me to make out words.

But now what scares me isn't the thought of the mob breaking in here. It's that, with all the clamor they're making,

I can't hear what that damp, speechless chimera is doing on the far side of the door.

"Aah—aah," it sighs. So it does have a voice, though barely. It sounds muddy and strangled. "Aah—aah. Dah—lan."

Oh, God. It's trying to say my name.

"Aah—aah. Dah—lan."

Ada, darling. That's what the blue mouthed at me that time in the woods.

Maybe the blue sent this thing to me: another of its *children*. I breathe in, deep, trying to calm myself, to loosen my bunched muscles and slow my heart. *It's just another chimera,* I tell myself. *It's not that different from me.*

"Yes," I say. "I'm Ada. Are you here to help me?"

There's a horrible squelching sound at the door. What is it doing? A few wet, babbling sighs. A long jiggling.

And then the lock pops open, and the doorknob turns. The door falls back, and I see it standing there: seven feet tall and greenish, with strange, bowed legs. It has huge, rounded, muscular thighs, but its arms are scrawny and crooked. A sort-of-human face with a mouth stretched across both cheeks and long pale eyes that wrap around the sides of its head. It's naked, wide-bodied, reeking of salt and seaweed; gills on its neck flutter with each exhalation. If I'm forty-five out of forty-six, this thing might be about twenty-three.

It gawks at me, sad and wistful and terrified, even though it could probably kill me with a single kick. Then it turns and shuffles up the hall without a backwards glance. A moment later, I run after it.

"Hey," I say, reaching for its soft pale arm. "Hey, wait! I didn't even get a chance to thank you. And I want to know who you are. The blue sent you, right?"

It aims a befuddled look at me, and its shuffle turns into a kind of hopping lope. It's going pretty fast now, and I trot to catch up. I'm not sure it understands a word I'm saying.

"Where did you come from?" I try. "Why haven't we seen you before?"

Then I get it: those underwater caves Rowan explored. He said there was more in them than just the bioluminescence everywhere; he just never told me *what* he'd seen. And I was too much of a coward to ask him.

Just like with my dad's messages, I was scared to know, and it makes me furious with myself. I've kept talking about how I want to speak the truth, know the truth, but when it's been right in front of me, I haven't wanted to look at it.

The greenish chimera darts around bends, and I keep following it, though it shoots me annoyed glances now and then over its shoulder. Where is everyone? I can't hear voices, not even the fizz coming through the loudspeakers at the gate. The banging has stopped, too. I think we're heading for the lobby.

"If those people outside break in here, you should head straight back to your cave, okay? I don't think they'll ever find you there."

It breaks into a springing run, long feet curling like

soft hooks at every step. There's no way I can keep up, but I try anyway, sprinting after it around the scarred mahogany check-in counter and into the lobby. Cold, rain-flecked wind whips into my face.

The picture window is completely shattered. Shards of aquamarine glass mound on the floor, and the sea looks raw and wild and somehow much too close. Points like crystal teeth edge the empty frame where the window used to be.

The chimera that freed me is already through, leaping across the meadow.

Did the mob already break in here, then? Is everyone hiding? I can't let myself think about any possibilities worse than that. Besides, if that mob had come rampaging through, wouldn't I have heard something?

If I take down Marley's chrysalis, will I be able to carry her by myself, hide with her in the hollow where Rowan and I saw the tadpoles? I'd be too afraid of tearing her covering if I tried to drag her.

I hesitate for half a moment, sick with everything I don't know, everything that might have happened while I was imprisoned and unconscious. Then I clamber over the heap of glass, hearing its awful soprano crunch, and outside.

Clouds sag overhead like a collapsing tent, and the rain twists and snaps.

Still nobody. Just grass thrashing in the wind. Beach roses and a few tattered daisies.

I realize what I was afraid of seeing out here: bodies. I walk forward, confused, gazing at the wild sea. Lightning flashes, and for an instant, the fence and its loops of razor wire reflect the light like a streak of diamonds.

There's something on the beach, deep in the shadow under that grassy shelf. A long ragged line, mostly hidden by the jutting rocks and tall grass in the way, and dark enough that I didn't notice it at first. I can't tell what it is, but it's moving.

Footsteps pound behind me, but high up. I turn just in time to see Ophelia launching herself off the roof, her wings in a savage whirl. She flies, or almost, and lands just beside me.

I flinch. She's been reporting on me. She was the one they sent to search our room, and she's probably convinced I've been spying on her, too.

"Ada! Ada, you know I tried to stop you from getting mixed up in everything here! But you wouldn't listen, or somehow I couldn't make you understand, and now you probably hate me. I didn't know what else to do, but I swear —I didn't understand in time how bad it would be."

I'm just wondering what she was doing up on the roof when the loudspeaker turns back on. A rough voice blasts through the static. "Fifteen minutes. We're waiting the way we agreed, but we won't give you any longer than that. Fifteen more minutes to show us, or we're coming in."

She jumps and clutches at me. "Ada, what are you thinking? You can't just stand here! You have to hide!"

But there was such a long stretch of silence before this!

"I hoped they had gone, the mob out there! It was quiet. Ophelia, what—"

"You're not listening to me! You need to run! Go, before he comes out and finds you!"

"But the normals—they've been staying away—Ophelia, why are they here now? What do they want?"

She stares at me like I'm insane, then starts shoving me down the slope, her thin arms taut and her wings beating into a blur. I stumble a little. "They came for you! Ada, go!"

"But if they came for me"—what sense does that make, though?—"shouldn't I go to the gate? Ophelia, you know I'll go with them if that's the only way to protect everyone!"

Even while I'm talking, part of me thinks, *Oh, really? Why should I?* And another part answers with a tumble of images: Indigo crying against my legs, Rowan's sad smile, and even Ophelia as she is right now, pushing me down the meadow in the dusky light, her black eyes glittering in their complicated way. But maybe I've gotten better at understanding the expression in them, because I could swear she's worried. About me.

"Ada, you can't do that! You're supposed to be dead! That's what Gabriel and Ms. Stuart told them. That you died yesterday in an accident. If they see you alive, they'll go berserk."

"But—why do they even want me?"

She's given up pushing me now. It's obvious that I'm not going anywhere until I get at least a few answers. Ophelia stops, breathing hard, and leans her head on my shoulder.

"Your dad, Ada. After he talked to Ms. Stuart, he went into town and started telling everyone in the bars that you're a normal human girl, and that we'd kidnapped you and brainwashed you. I think he thought it was the only way to get you back."

"But if they think I'm dead, then —"

"They don't believe it, Ada."

"Ophelia, I don't understand!"

"So Gabriel told them we'd show them the body! He said he and Martin found your body an hour ago, and they were going to pull it up from the cave."

Now I understand. I don't think Ophelia's eyes can cry, but her breath comes in rapid sobs. *Really? Ms. Stuart would let that happen?*

Maybe she would. If she thought it was a choice between killing me and watching all the other kids here die, probably she'd tell herself she had no choice. She thinks I know things that would destroy them if they let me leave here alive. What did she say when Rowan was missing? That she didn't have the *luxury* of worrying too much about my safety?

"Ada, I don't know — his ankle's still slowing him down — and maybe he and Martin decided to search the building first, but any second now they'll look out here. Please just go."

Where's Rowan? I want to ask. But now it's sinking in: there's no time to ask anything. I nod and turn to run, toward the woods or toward the water. Maybe, just maybe, Soraya will come for me again.

I turn, and whatever it was I saw on the beach isn't there

anymore. I do a double take and then spot it again, a long dark formation advancing through the rusty grass. They're squeezed so close together, and it's getting so dark, that it takes even me a moment to understand what I'm seeing: a hundred human-shaped bodies with heads outlined by the tarnished glow of the sea.

A small army, it looks like, and they're coming toward us. I hear myself cry out.

Ophelia turns to follow my gaze, and screams.

CHAPTER THIRTY

COLD, THEY'RE SO COLD. I forget about running and stare at them, fascinated: I've never seen a group of human-looking bodies with no red glow in my life. I've never seen people who look like a swarm of shadows in the twilight, but this must be what everyone else sees all the time. Even the air is warmer than they are; I guess they're still chilled from the sea.

"Ada! It's them! It's the mob! I don't know how, but somehow they got through the fence!" Ophelia is twisting in panic, not sure which way to go, and one wing slaps at my arm. I think she's flapping unconsciously.

"No. It's something else. I don't think they're here to hurt us, Ophelia."

"What are you *talking* about?"

"They're cold. Cold-blooded. They've just—gone beyond what we are."

She gives a strange, sobbing laugh. I'm not sure she believes me.

"Ada? There's something I have to tell you. I did something I knew was wrong. Gabriel said — but I shouldn't have listened to him. Please don't hate me. I'm really sorry."

I turn to her. She's staring at me, and the glitter of her eyes seems quicker than usual, even desperate. "I wasn't spying for my dad, Ophelia. I would never do that."

"I know that now. For a while I let Gabriel convince me, but I don't think — in my heart I knew it wasn't true. Oh, Ada, no!" She isn't looking at me anymore, but behind me, toward that maw of broken glass that used to be the lobby window. I start to turn.

And that's when something big, heavy, and huffing comes slamming through the air and knocks me flat on my face. A heavy body drops on top of mine, its hard wings clacking. Meaty hands on arms with too many joints pin my wrists to the ground. They're glowing bright red, like he has a fever.

"Bad, bad Ada. Thinks she's a normal human. Thinks I'm no good, but she's the bad, horrible, sneaking liar. She has to die. Now. But I'm sad to kill you, Ada." He gets both my wrists in one hand, and his free hand moves down. He must be reaching for my throat. I try to struggle, but he's too heavy.

"Martin, let her go!" Ophelia aims a vicious kick at him, but he's so bulky and she's so fragile that he barely grunts.

"You're really pretending you care what happens to Ada?" Gabriel's voice asks from somewhere pretty close by. He almost sounds like he thinks it's funny, but in a cold, numb way. "After what you did to her?"

Martin moves so he has one knee pressed between my shoulder blades and his hand across my mouth. All at once I understand: he's not planning to strangle me. That leaves too many obvious marks that the human mob would notice. He's breathing heavily, maybe crying, as he works up the nerve to snap my neck.

That's something they can say happened by accident.

Ophelia gives a shriek and flings herself on Martin, but this time she doesn't seem to be punching him. I can't quite tell, but I think she's got her hands on his back, prying at something. He lets out a high, shocked grunt, and his grip loosens. "Ophelia! Don't hurt my wings!"

"Let Ada go, or I'll tear them right off!"

The kime army is close enough now that I can hear the rubbery flapping of their feet. With all the drama going on, I think Gabriel hadn't even noticed them, but he does now. My face is crushed into the grass, so I can't see what's happening, but I hear his sudden intake of breath. It's dark enough that I wonder if he's making the same mistake Ophelia did, thinking they're human.

Martin sort of reels back in confusion, trying to shake off Ophelia. He's still straddling me, but at least my hands are free again, and I can push myself up enough to look around. This time I think I see a sliver of red glowing way back in the crowd of bodies, but what sense does that make?

Then Martin sees them too and starts making a low, terrified babbling.

Because they're all around us now. One swoops down without breaking his stride, grabs Gabriel by the knees, and swings him over his shoulder. Gabriel screams and flails, but it doesn't do him any good. They look more or less like the chimera that opened the door for me, tall and pallid and greenish, but there are variations—like somebody was trying to come up with the perfect saltwater frog person and wanted to see which way worked best.

One of them grabs Martin by the back of his neck and casually flings him into the grass. Those scrawny arms they have are stronger than they look. I'm struggling to my feet, soft green skin sticking to me and slurping free again with every passing touch—and then I get scooped up too, but a lot more gently than Gabriel was. One of the kimes has me wadded up in its arms the way a little kid would smoosh a pet cat. I don't see Ophelia, but she must be here somewhere.

And now the metallic crashing is starting again: louder, steadier, more determined. In a jumbled way, I understand that the mob is working seriously to batter down the gate. And after what those people did to the scientists at Novasphere, how can I think that they won't do the same to us?

I hear a chorus of screams starting at the bottom of the hill, then breaking apart. Some of the kids are running for it, off to hide the best they can in the woods or the water—but except for Rowan, probably nobody has much hope of getting out of here. Can anyone else dive deep enough to get through that hole?

Rowan. Where *is* he?

There's one thing that mob isn't expecting, though, and it's the mass of amphibious kimes carrying me and Gabriel. As we sweep over the top of the hill and start charging down, one thing is absolutely clear: that's where we're going. The gate.

Maybe Gabriel *is* about to get the war he's always wanted. Maybe most of us, human and chimera, are going to die tonight, torn and stabbed and wallowing in blood. Will I see stars in the horror like Dr. Jacoway did?

Then something hits me. "Marley," I gasp to the chimera holding me. "She can't run. She can't move at all by herself. But you and your friends — you can carry her to the cave? You have to help her!"

"Aah — aah," it says. From its tone I can tell that it's trying to calm me, hush me. "Aahd — aah. No. Not Maar — lah."

That's the closest they've come to really speaking, but it's enough for me to know that they can learn to say English words — and also that this kime can understand me. It knows who I am, and it knows who Marley is, too.

"Not Marley? How can you say that? She's helpless, and she's — your sister! You can't let them hurt her."

It looks down at me, sharply. The movement of its run shakes through my body, but there's just enough light for me to see the reproach in its eyes. "Not. Hurt. Maar — lah."

"You're saying no one will hurt her?" I ask. But it's not looking at me anymore. It's gazing ahead to the gate, and when I turn that way, I see the night broken by streaking headlamps and floodlights. I hear the methodical booming of a heavy truck, squealing back and then slamming forward again and again. Bodies like red flames in a gust, jumping and fearful and ready to blaze higher; from here I can't tell which ones are humans and which are chimeras.

Then I hear the violent, wrenching roar as the gate finally gives way.

CHAPTER THIRTY-ONE

T HE HEADLIGHTS thrust forward, twisting on the blackberry bushes. The normals are driving right onto the grounds, their voices tumbling out in drunken shouts and bursts of ugly laughter. I think most of the kids have scattered by now, but I can hear Ms. Stuart trying to shout the invaders down, and Dr. Jacoway—oh, he's singing to himself, his voice slurred and dreamy and utterly insane.

Red-shining bodies rush staggering over the grass. I see Dr. Jacoway holding up his arms, waving them back and forth.

"Not the children! You have no business, sirs, in tampering with miracles you could never understand. But, oh, I understand! I know these children for what they are. The spirit of life itself saw the coming risk of human extinction, and it made them, it made them to be our new hope!" The words come out as a weird, warped song, and he walks right into the path of a truck rumbling slowly onto the grounds, the same one that was here before, with the loudspeakers in the back.

Ms. Stuart must be close enough to see what's happening. Why doesn't she run to him and drag him out of its way? "I will not allow it. Not a hair, not a scale, not one feather. I will not! I will—"

"Dr. Jacoway!" I scream. "They're not stopping!"

But he doesn't hear me, or he doesn't care. He's still singing as the truck rolls over him. I see him pulled under the wheels, I hear his breathy cry, and I'm struggling to free myself from the kime carrying me. To help him. But I can't.

I hear his song end.

In the darkness and confusion, the stampeding humans don't seem to notice us until we're pretty close. The mob is bigger than last time, but even so, I'm pretty sure the frog chimeras have them seriously outnumbered. There's a burst of light, maybe from a flashlight, and a strange woman's face jerks to a halt inches from mine. Her mouth is wide, her hair sticking up and singed off on one side. She's gawking at the kime holding me and trying to scream, but all she can make are these little gagging sounds.

But other people can still scream, and they do.

I hear gunshots, and I watch as one of the greenish kimes swipes a gun out of someone's hand without even looking and drives it barrel-first into the ground.

Bright orange light flares through the grass, and then I realize that a man with a torch has been snatched up by his ankles so that the fire laps up around his arm. He shrieks and drops the torch, and the kime holding him treads out the fire with its bare damp feet.

I can hear the hiss as the flames are extinguished. I'd like to believe it doesn't hurt, but the pale semihuman face is tight with pain.

But it doesn't do anything to the man it's gripping. His upside-down face is red and sweating, and his arms swing out in random, pointless punches. But the kime just lets him dangle, and my heart speeds up from hope: that the kime army has come here to stop them. To protect all of us.

Not to hurt anyone, even if they might deserve it. Not to fight.

Another of the frog people wrests a megaphone from a teenage human boy who's just sitting on the ground in shock, and hands it politely to someone back behind us. I crane, but I can't see who it is.

The chaos seems to be dying down. Maybe half the human mob has run away. The truck and a few pickups and cars are so tightly surrounded by silent green chimeras that they've stopped trying to drive. And the remaining normals are mostly caught by their feet or pinned in the grass. There's a feeling of weary confusion in the air. Nobody knows what to do with a riot that has stopped before it could really get going —even if it's stopped too late for Dr. Jacoway.

Someone climbs on top of a car and hefts the megaphone.

"You said you came for Ada Lahey. She's here, and she's fine, and she can leave with you. If she wants to. No one will stop her."

Rowan. He's the glimpse of warmth I saw before, squeezed

in with the frog people. That's where he was: he went to get help.

The chimera holding me sets me softly on my feet.

"The normal girl," someone says, jumping down from the truck carrying the loudspeakers. I recognize him. It's the man who was doing the talking the first night, when they threw a rock at me. Scott Held, Gabriel said, one of the leaders of the massacre at Novasphere, and now he's murdered the last survivor from that night. Dr. Jacoway's mind was shattered, I know that. And so was his heart.

But his courage and his kindness? Those were as strong and intact as ever.

"The normal girl," Scott Held repeats, walking toward me. His dark hair crests in the wind. He must have been young when he killed those scientists, because he doesn't look older than his early thirties now. "We should have known as soon as we saw you, that you couldn't be one of these freaks. We never should have been fooled. You know they lied and told us you were dead? We know better now, Ada, better about all of it, and we're here to get you out."

He reaches for me. I pull away. How dare this man act like he's my personal hero?

"Don't touch me," I say.

"She's just frightened," somebody croons. A woman. "The poor girl is in shock. Get her father, somebody, will you? He's in the car just back around the bend."

So my dad told the lies that started this mess, but then

he decided to wait it out at a safe distance? He didn't want to watch the kids here die because of him?

"We'll take her and go peacefully," Scott announces to the kime army, like he's got anything to say about it. They stand still and watch him, a few of them holding human captives—though most of the humans have been set down now and are leaning on each other or huddling in the grass. "We'll overlook—whatever this new freak show is, that you've all been getting up to." He nods to indicate the frog chimeras, and he doesn't even try to keep the disgust off his face. "As long as we never see anything that there shouldn't be outside the grounds. Anything unnatural."

I can tell from his voice that he's lying. They're outnumbered now, but he's already plotting to come back. Maybe with more powerful weapons. Maybe with the real military. And he's so sure everyone hates us that he's not even worried about going to prison for what he's done.

"I'm as unnatural as they are," I say. "If I can leave here, then so can everyone else."

"Now, Ada, that's not true. They've told you so many lies that you've started believing them. But you're a real, right, pure-human little girl, and this is no place for you."

I never like being condescended to very much, but I like it even less from someone who just murdered my friend—because even if Dr. Jacoway couldn't remember me for ten minutes at a stretch, that's exactly what he was.

"I can prove what I am," I say. "And I'm not ashamed of it."

I keep waiting for Ms. Stuart to say something, but she's

watching from off to the side and keeping her mouth shut. She's smart. Probably she's calculating that anything she can say will just make the situation worse for her. Now that she's been caught lying, it's not a good idea to call attention to herself.

Gabriel's nearby too, face-down on the ground with a frog chimera sitting languidly on his back. His visible skin is blinking like a traffic light, but no one is paying attention.

Rowan is the one who comes to me. He climbs down off his perch, the megaphone dangling from his hand, and twists his way through the tangle of humans and chimeras. His fur makes his red glow look softer and fuzzier than most people's. When he gets close, Scott Held jumps back from us, looking at Rowan's round, silky head with absolute loathing.

Rowan reaches a flipper toward my cheek and then drops it self-consciously. His brown eyes are riveted on mine.

"Ada," he half whispers. He leans closer. "Ada, this is your chance to get out, and you should take it. You know what Gabriel would have — no one here *deserves* to have you stay."

"You deserve it," I tell him. "And so does Soraya."

"Just — go have a normal life, Ada. No one could ever guess, not by looking at you. Don't give up your whole future for us!" Tears are wobbling in his dark eyes. One slips free and soaks into the fur on his neck.

I have more than one possible future, though. It's not about giving up my old ideas of my future; it's about choosing a new future, one I'm just beginning to understand. But I don't have time to explain that to Rowan now. I can see a section of the road through the broken gate, and my dad is there, running around the bend. Once he gets here and starts talking, I probably won't be able to get anyone to listen to me. They'll trust him instead. I might be carried out of here by force.

I turn to Scott Held. "Do you have a piece of paper? Or your jacket would work, too. Hold it up in front of one hand."

There's a wave of murmuring from the humans. The frog chimeras are just as quiet as ever. Rowan is tear-streaked and pink, like he's holding his breath. "Why?" Scott Held asks. He's too taken aback to keep simpering at me.

"So I can show you how *unnatural* I am."

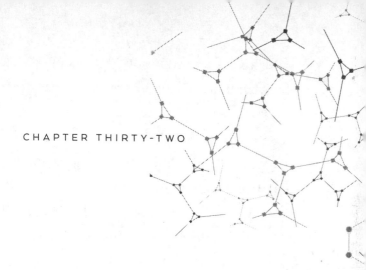

CHAPTER THIRTY-TWO

I T ONLY takes half a minute. Scott Held and his followers might not want to believe it, but they all know that nobody human could see what I can see. Only a filthy, hideous kime could do that. Rowan steps out of the way but stays close, letting me know he's there for me. I stare them down. "Well?"

And that's when my dad comes pounding through the gate, sparing just one quick glance for the bent iron bars. He doesn't seem interested in the frog chimeras at all. Just how much did he know before I came here?

"Ada! Ada, thank God you're safe. What unbelievable cruelty—they told me you were dead, sweetheart. I knew it couldn't be true."

He's been coming closer while he's talking, and now he reaches to pull me into his arms. I step back before he can catch me.

"Ms. Stuart lied to you," I say. "But you lied, too. Did you know Dr. Jacoway? You're both biologists. Did you ever meet him?"

"Dr. Jacoway?" He looks stunned, and really sweet, with his golden-brown skin and warm gaze and his glasses tipped at a slant. I don't think I understood how badly I missed him and my mom and my home until this moment. All I want to do is give in, hug him tight and sob while he carries me to the car. But I can't. "I studied under him. Many years ago."

"He's dead," I say. "Scott Held crushed him to death with his truck. And he was murdered because he wanted to protect the kids here. Not because he'd done anything wrong." Dad stares at me. "You ran past his body, and you didn't even look."

"I was desperate to reach you, sweetheart. Once they made that outrageous claim, that you'd been killed in an accident—I wasn't sure what they'd try next. I was sure you were in danger."

He steps forward again, and again I dance out of reach. My hair keeps blowing in my face, and when I push it back, my cheeks are slippery with tears. I didn't even know I was crying.

"I was. Gabriel over there tried to murder me, twice. And the second time Ms. Stuart was ready to sit back and let it happen."

I know they're both listening, but I won't look at them. They're no better than Scott Held; just like him, they'll crush anyone in the way of their plans.

And right now I can't look at my dad, either. I love him,

but I understand too much. I know what he's done. I turn my head toward the violet sky, the black trees pitching like waves. Bats like shining ribbons swoop after insects.

I need to cry for hours in someone's arms, but they won't be his.

"That's just what I was afraid of. So you can see — Ada, you accuse me of lying, and I did. I would have said anything, done *anything* I had to, to get you out of here!"

"Maybe you should have thought about that," I say, "before you sent me in here to be your spy."

The crowd has been pretty quiet. I guess for them, watching this is as good as TV. But now there are some reactions: surprised huffs and murmuring. My dad glances around. Like he was counting on me to keep that part secret and not embarrass him.

Like that matters more than all the kids who could have died tonight. More than Dr. Jacoway, lying there with his rib cage crushed and his mouth wide open. I can't see him well —there are too many people in the way—but I can see his ruby glow starting to dim to a dull brick red.

"I never wanted it to be you, Ada," my dad says at last. The same words he used in his email. "But my bosses, my—associates—all impressed on me how perfect you were for the task. So beautifully human-looking that no one would question how you'd passed undetected for so long."

So it was never a secret that I'm a chimera—at least, it wasn't a secret from everyone. It's a crazy thing to realize. Maybe I was only free all those years because his *associates* were waiting for me to be old enough to be their pawn. Maybe during all those doctors' visits they were studying me, and I never even guessed. There's a much bigger game being played than I ever realized. If there's some kind of conspiracy, how deep does it really go? My breath is heaving, and I must look stunned.

I guess he doesn't notice how much understanding this hurts me, because he just keeps talking.

"But then, if you came under suspicion — if they thought you were a human plant — you could easily prove your true nature." I think of Ms. Stuart, fake-casually asking me for that demonstration in her office. She'd wondered that exact thing. "And then, there's your extraordinary vision. It's unique, as far as we know."

There it is again. I wonder if he wanted the same thing Ms. Stuart did: for me to find the blue, and find a way to help him use it. Harness its power, like it's just some weapon and the first side that gets hold of it will win. I can see how people who've never experienced the blue for themselves might get that idea, and how amazing it would be to control the force that made all of us. But nobody can *use* it; it has its own ideas. That doesn't seem to occur to either of them.

And they can't use me, either.

"Why did you *agree* to send me, though? What did they promise you? You said something about leaving Long Island, but that — you wouldn't have agreed just for that?"

He flushes. The heat of his blood rising in his cheeks

makes them shine like lanterns. That's enough of an answer. Right; being stuck in the quarantined zone has been *devastating* for his career.

"The whole test," I say. "The Popsicles. You were in on the plan before that happened. You helped set me up. And you let me believe I was contagious, but you knew that wasn't true, either."

"Ada," he says. "Ada, listen. I wanted what was best for you. For our whole family. Staying inside the quarantine — it's *stifling*. I wanted a better future than that for you."

"And what about Marley and Corbin?" I ask. "They got caught too. Ripped away from their families. Why? Just to make the whole bust look more realistic?"

He doesn't answer that. Not directly. "Marley? We'd been watching that girl for years. I posed as a pediatrician to study her personally, once; such a fascinating case. She's only thirty-seven out of forty-six. Barely human at all. It's astounding that she was able to pass for so long."

The answer that matters to me isn't in his words. It's in the tone of his voice. There's a thin, sharp edge of contempt.

I'm forty-five out of forty-six, and I guess that makes me almost good enough. *Almost* a real daughter. But not quite so real that he wasn't willing to trade me for his freedom. I see. I completely understand, and I wish more than anything that I could squeeze all my love for him out of my heart. Crush it and throw it on the grass and tell him to his face that I hate him.

But I can't. And I don't. I love him, and I just wish he'd done a better job of loving me back.

He reaches toward me again. "Ada, come along. I understand you feel strongly about the choices I made, and you have every right to be upset. Let's talk about this at home."

His voice has softened so quickly that it's like he threw a switch. He knows how to say all the right things. He's smart that way. But Ms. Stuart is pretty good at that too.

Rowan, out of everybody — he's the only one who recognizes just how awful this is. He leans closer and curls a flipper on my shoulder.

"Dr. Lahey? You're welcome to visit here — I mean, if Ada wants to see you. But there's no way we'll let you take Ada against her will."

My dad scowls at him. "And who do you mean by *we?* You and the people who tried to murder her?"

Rowan shakes his head. "They don't count anymore. And anyway, you know that's not who I meant."

As the night gets deeper, the tall greenish army blends into the darkness more. But as I look around, I realize they've moved to stand in a ring twenty feet from me and Rowan. They're guarding us. My dad stares at them and then turns around, probably checking to see how many of Scott Held's people he can call on for support.

The answer is almost none. They've been getting up off the ground in ones and twos, staring around disoriented, and then wandering off. Why would anybody stay to fight over a kime girl like me? Back through the gate, back into cars. Hot exhaust plumes scarlet from their tailpipes. Even Scott Held is climbing back into the cab of his truck and slamming the door. His mouth is bent in a disappointed sneer.

My dad turns back to me. There's such a strange look on his face: regret and longing, but also something more calculating, like he's about to lose something he wants intensely. And I think I can guess what it is. He still needs me and whatever I know to persuade his bosses to let him leave Long Island.

"I'm not going anywhere," I say, just to make sure that's clear. "I still love you and Mom. But I would never do what you asked me to do. You expected me to betray everybody here, and you don't even know who they are."

Like Soraya. If she's my sister, my twin, then she's also his daughter, in a way. And he might not even know she exists. It feels like too much to explain right now, though.

But maybe he'll visit. Maybe I'll be able to forgive him. And once I know I can trust him again, maybe I'll take him to meet her.

"Ada," he says. The look in his eyes is brighter now. Hungrier. "Ada, did you *see* it?"

Is that all he cares about? "I've seen it. We've — communicated, a little. But I don't know what it is."

"No one knows. Not really." He smiles ruefully. "We don't know what it wants, or why it chose Long Island as the site for its newest experiments. We can only guess. If you ask me, I'd speculate that it's the reason for all the sudden jumps in the evolutionary record. I'd say it's the vital intelligence of Earth itself. The will to life, bubbling over into a sentient being. Imagine what we could do if we could master that!"

He looks around at the frog people, and I know what he sees in them.

Potential. *Power.* Anyone who can conduct the force that made them could choose the future for our whole planet.

"It wouldn't let you," I say. "It does what it wants to do." I don't think he believes me, though, any more than Ms. Stuart would. "Why didn't you just tell me the truth, though, before you sent me here? You could have explained. You could have told me you needed a spy in here, and *asked* me how I felt about that. Instead you put on this huge act." It's still sinking in.

Every word he said was a lie. Even when he said, *Our daughter is staying with her family,* he was just waiting for me to contradict him and insist on coming here instead. He was so sure he could predict every last thing I would do. He was counting on it.

But he was only right about some of it. At first I went along with his script just perfectly, but then I started to slide off into choices he hadn't imagined.

"Why didn't I tell you? Because I knew that, unless your initial reactions were completely authentic, you'd give yourself away. You're such a fundamentally honest person, Ada, dearest. You're such a terrible liar."

I'd thought I was done being surprised, but he's smiling in a way that lets me know he means it.

He reaches out one more time and strokes my cheek, and

now I don't pull away from him. But I don't go to him, either. I need more time to get past the bitterness before I can treat him like he's really my dad again. Dr. Jacoway died because of all the lies my dad told. I can't just ignore that.

Even though he's crying now. "Ada. You really won't come with me? I can arrange to keep you unregistered. We can explain to the school that the lab made a mistake and that you've been cleared. No one will ever suspect you aren't entirely human."

I don't care anymore who knows what I am. That's not the point at all. If it's safe to let me live around humans, if he's so sure of that, why should any of us stay shut away from the world?

"I won't leave here," I say. "Not until all of us can, without anybody trying to hurt us. And not until there's some kind of justice for Dr. Jacoway! Do you think that's ever going to happen?"

Rowan lets out a long huff of air, like he's been holding his breath all this time, and pulls me into a hug. The fur on his shoulder is thick and warm, and soon it's damp with my tears.

CHAPTER THIRTY-THREE

THE KIDS start to drift back now that it's quiet. They stop in the deepest shadows of the trees, watching cautiously. They stare at the kime army and then at the steel gate, its bars warped and one side halfway ripped from its hinges. Most of them have been locked up in here since they were babies, but now a few of the braver ones start slipping through the gate in pairs, making short exploratory forays up the road. Small feathered hands hold small spiny claws, and their voices float to me in excited whispers.

I should stop holding Rowan. I haven't forgotten my promise to Soraya, and I know it's not fair to him, either. But for now I can't let go. He's stroking my hair, and my back is trembling. "Ada, it's going to be okay. I can't believe you did that, but it's okay. We'll figure it all out."

"I'm afraid this doesn't change anything, Rowan." Oh, now that the mob has gone, Ms. Stuart feels like it's up to her to say what's changed. *Everything* has changed. Why isn't that obvious to her? "Don't you see? That touching scene we just witnessed was all a masquerade. Theater meant to persuade us that Ada was unjustly accused. But she's still a spy, and we still have to take steps to prevent her from harming us."

Rowan squeezes me tighter and glares at her. "That's crazy."

The greenish chimeras open their mouths just a little and emit wet hisses. The circle steps in closer, and Ms. Stuart glances at them nervously, like maybe she's just understood that they'll follow Rowan's lead. Not hers.

"Not Aah—ahh," one says distinctly. I think it's my friend from before, the one who scooped me up and carried me here. A lot of them look sort of alike to me, but there's a tiny notch in its upper lip that I remember.

"The letter, Rowan. When Ophelia found it in Ada's duffle, the envelope was torn open. Ada's whole pretense that she had no idea what her father expected of her—that was all a lie. She knew perfectly all along."

I'm so surprised I can't react at first. I pull away from Rowan, and there's a trace of doubt in his eyes. It's faint, but I can still see it.

"I never even *unzipped* my duffle! I just shoved it into a drawer. I was afraid that there would be something in there —whatever it was—that would be too upsetting."

I turn to Ms. Stuart. Her upper lip hikes, and her eyes are wounded and cold. She believes what she's saying. "That isn't what Ophelia told us, Ada."

Gabriel's gotten up behind her, his skin silvery and faintly luminous. His bioluminescence forms a moonlike glaze over his body heat. He's watching Rowan's face, his lips pressed tightly together, not saying a word. Just waiting to see how it plays out. And all at once I know what Ophelia was about to confess earlier, when she said she'd done something wrong.

"Where is she?" I'm scanning the field. In the darkness her wings should be easy to spot, like shining gossamer, but I can't find her anywhere. "I think she might say something different if you ask her again."

A wave of anxiety passes over Gabriel's face, and with it a spurt of emerald static. I can tell he's trying to suppress his colors, but he doesn't manage it in time. Not before Rowan sees it.

"Of course Ophelia's going to change her story," Gabe snarls. He nods at the frog chimeras. "She'll be scared to death, with your freak squad there threatening her."

I can't believe he just said that — the pro-chimera militant himself? "Did you just call them *freaks*? They're exactly like us!"

Maybe not exactly, though. They aren't as human. I think they must be what those tadpole creatures grow up to be. And all at once, I understand something.

"Actually, the blue made them after us," I say. "We were just the first experiment. A trial run. I bet they're — more *advanced* than we are, and they just grow up faster than we do. They can live underwater as well as in the air, for one thing.

And that's why there are so many of the same kind. The blue was happier with how they'd turned out!"

Rowan ignores all of this. "Gabriel? What have you done?"

I can see Gabe falter, just a little bit. One thing I'm sure of: he cares, a lot, how Rowan feels about him. Pale, nervous blue stutters on his skin, but then he gets his attitude together again. "You really believe I did something to your girlfriend there?"

Rowan flinches. "She's not my girlfriend. And whether she is or not, it's not okay to pressure Ophelia to lie about her!"

"Gabriel?" That's Ms. Stuart. This honestly never occurred to her, I can tell.

"You got Ophelia to say that," Rowan persists, "so that when you told Ms. Stuart Ada had to die, she'd decide you were right. Like, that there was no other choice. If she was *sure* Ada was spying, you could persuade her it was too dangerous to keep Ada alive. Gabriel, why? When you attacked her before, Ada said you did it to get me back. To trade her to Soraya for me. I didn't like it, but at least it made sense!"

Ms. Stuart actually staggers a little in shock, but I don't much care what she's going through. Because balanced at the very summit of the treetops to my right, I notice a soft disturbance: something red and fluttering, like poppy petals in the wind. I would have seen it earlier if I'd thought of looking up so far.

"Ophelia's in the trees," I say. "Over there." I point, but in the darkness I don't know if anyone but me will see her. The clouds are still thick, and there's no trace of starlight. "And she's higher up than I think anyone could climb."

Even after everything that's happened, I'm so excited for her. How did she get up there if she didn't truly fly?

Ms. Stuart lets out a long exhalation. There's so much grief in the sound of it that I start to feel sorry for her after all. "I clearly need her input. She appears to be the only one who can tell me what happened here." She turns and shouts toward the trees, "Ophelia! Ophelia, can you hear me? We need you."

The red petal shapes stop moving completely. For a long moment, they hold perfectly still, and even from here, I can tell what it means. Ophelia would give anything to avoid having to talk about what she did.

She's ashamed. And my breath catches in my throat. I desperately need Ophelia to tell the truth. If she doesn't, it's going to be unbearable for me to live here, but that's not the only reason. It's for her sake, too.

If Ophelia betrays me again, there's a part of her that will never recover.

I watch her balancing on the highest tip of the tree. She gives a hesitant wobble and pauses, and the air in my throat feels hard and jagged. I want to believe in her. I want to forget she ever told that lie, but no matter how hard I wish those things, I can't make this choice for her.

Then she leaps, and the ruby blur of her wings streaks the dark clouds.

She flies down—she really flies!—and stops to hover directly above us. "Ada," she says. "Ada, you know? They told you?"

"I know," I tell her. "But I don't care at all, Ophelia. Not if you tell everyone the truth now." She still looks uncertain, sort of teetering in midair. "I promise. I'll never bring it up again."

She lands on the grass near us. The gust from her wing-beats sends my hair flying.

"I'm the one who opened the letter, Ms. Stuart." Her voice is very deliberate, and her black eyes sparkle like galaxies. "Gabriel told me we had to—that he was positive Ada was spying, but that we needed stronger evidence. I let him talk me into it, but I knew the whole time it was wrong. And I'm really sorry."

"You could have gotten Ada murdered!" Rowan snaps. Ms. Stuart has turned bone white, so tense she seems about to shatter.

"I know. I didn't realize—I mean, I never thought Gabe would do something that horrible. Once I heard him talking to Martin, though, I realized what it all meant. Ada, I tried to warn you!"

She leans away from me like she's afraid I'll hit her.

Ms. Stuart's stare drives at Gabriel, so wounded and accusing he steps back. His arms are wrapped tight around his chest.

"Ada *is* a spy," he announces, almost like he thinks he's

the one who's been treated unfairly. His skin strobes with indignation. "She *is* dangerous. She's been prying into everything, watching everything that goes on here! I knew what she was up to. I was totally onto her ever since she started talking about algae that time. I just didn't have proof."

"So you fabricated it." Ms. Stuart's voice sounds emptied, stunned. "Gabriel, I would do almost anything to advance our cause. But I draw the line at killing an innocent child."

"She's not innocent! That's what I'm telling you. She's been scheming and sneaking since she got here. Plotting to stop us. And now you're looking at me like I'm the problem! I was the only one *protecting* us."

He looks expectantly from her to Rowan, and Rowan steps close and wraps an arm around me. And after a moment Ophelia comes up on my other side and reaches to take my hand. I hear the crisp rustle of her wing against my shirt, and I give her hand a squeeze.

No matter what she did before, she came through for me when I needed her most. There have been so many times when I've doubted her, but maybe, just maybe, I can let go of that now.

"Gabriel, I know you don't believe it. But nobody here needs protecting from me. Just because I think what you and Ms. Stuart are doing is a huge mistake, that doesn't mean you need to treat me like I'm the enemy!"

"You're only staying so you can keep trying to ruin everything!" He sounds desperate, breathless. It's strange to realize that even if Gabriel has evil in him, he's genuinely convinced that he's doing the right thing—and doing it for all the chimeras. There aren't a lot of people who will fight for the kids here, and he's trying to be their champion.

It would be so much better if we didn't have to hate each other. That's all I can keep thinking, over and over. I've made up my mind to stay, and that means I can't just spit in Gabriel's face and walk away. I need him to understand.

"That's not it," I say. "Rowan knows why I'm staying."

Rowan tips his head. "I know one reason, anyway. If you mean what I think you mean."

Ms. Stuart sighs in loud exasperation. It's almost funny.

Rowan turns back to everyone. "Ada and Soraya have the exact same face. They must be some kind of twins—like, the human genes in Soraya *have* to be copied from Ada. I didn't want to say anything. Soraya's life is hard enough, and until I was sure everyone here could trust Ada—and until Ada trusted us—I didn't want Soraya getting mixed up in it. But she is. Do you have any idea how lonely Soraya's been all her life, with nobody she can talk to, ever, except me? Squids are just as weird about Soraya as humans are about us. If Ada left now, I think Soraya would be incredibly hurt."

Ms. Stuart nods. "Is that the truth, Ada? You don't want to leave Soraya?"

"That's part of it," I say. "The other part is what I told my dad. We should all be free together. We *will* be free, someday. I know we will, even if it takes a long time. And, Ms. Stuart?

There's a reason your algae die away from Long Island. The blue doesn't want Chimera Syndrome to spread anywhere else, at least not for now. If you really care about us, you'll stop trying to make that happen."

Gabriel snorts. And I think I get it. Their idea might be that if there are millions of chimeras being born all over the country, then people will be forced to accept us. Maybe they want *all* the children born to be chimeras, so that humanity will have to choose between us and just disappearing completely.

Maybe humans would give in then. Or they might forget about locking us up and just start slaughtering us at birth instead. It's a dangerous gamble he and Ms. Stuart are taking. Too dangerous. That's what the blue's been trying to say. That's why it's worried about its children.

Ms. Stuart stares. I think it's the first time she's really understood me, and it might be the first time I've understood her, too. There's a long pause. I can see all the contradictory thoughts and impulses churning in her eyes. I'm asking her to give up the biggest dream of her life.

"If your blue will communicate with me, I'm prepared to listen."

"I'll tell it you said so," I say. But actually I don't have to, because it's all around us now. It spreads itself wide enough to take in everyone, me and Rowan and Ophelia, the frog chimeras, Ms. Stuart and the littler kids chasing fireflies by the torn gate. Even Gabriel. We could all be floating together, leaves

caught in a storm of blue light: the blue of mallards, of iridescent butterflies, of a skydiver's spinning gaze.

The blue of beginnings.

I can tell Ms. Stuart feels it caressing her. Wonder lights
up her tired brown eyes.

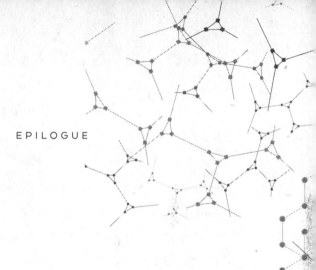

ROWAN'S DARK fur shines amber in the setting sun. He emits a groaning sound with five tongue clicks in the middle. He smiles at the girl with wet sand glazing her brown skin. "So, that's basically our word for a good possibility—for something we want to happen. You try it."

A row of pink seashells is balanced on each of Ada's thighs. She picks up another shell, examines it thoughtfully, and then adds it to her collection. Her first attempt to mimic his utterance comes out so strangely that they both burst out laughing.

"What about the word for a bad possibility? Is that easier?"

"Probably," Rowan says. His mouth falls, and he fixes his gaze on the waves. "Ada? I think that's what we're here for. The chimeras."

"How do you mean?"

"I mean—I'm pretty sure that's why the blue made us. In case of bad possibilities. Like, if humans hurt the planet too much, or start a nuclear war or something, then maybe enough of us would survive even if normal people couldn't. We'd be the ones to start over. Could you try asking it sometime if I'm right?"

Ada props herself on one elbow, and black waves cascade over her shoulder. Her skin glows with the falling light. Rowan glances at her and then carefully looks away again before Ada notices his gaze. "That sounds like what Dr. Jacoway said, right before he died. So, you think we're some kind of backup plan? If things ever get really bad? Like, chimeras are humanity *insurance?*"

"Yeah. I've thought about it a lot, and I'm almost positive. You know, the blue doesn't need Chimera Syndrome to spread everywhere just yet. It's fine with keeping us here— like, as a strategic reserve. It's experimenting with a bunch of different kinds of part humans, that could maybe survive different problems? It makes total sense. And then we really do have a purpose."

"Even if regular humans don't appreciate it?" Ada smiles so warmly at him that he flushes.

"Maybe that doesn't matter. We're here if the world ever needs us. We can carry on—well, hopefully just the good parts of being human."

Ada shakes her head. "We don't have just the good parts."

"I know. Or I wouldn't have had to go racing to those undersea chimeras to stop Gabe from killing you." Rowan pauses. "But they rushed to help as soon as I asked them, and maybe that proves we have *enough* of the good parts in us? I mean, to make the whole project worthwhile?"

"You're calling us a *project?*" Ada laughs. "That makes it sound like the blue stuck us together with tape. Like, for a science fair or something. Tape and fur and wings and tentacles."

Rowan grins back and gives the same call again, a long groan broken by five rapid clicks. *A good possibility.*

A flurry of wings breaks the air over their heads, and Ophelia thuds down in a spray of sand. "Ada! Rowan! You have to come right now! This second! It's—oh, she's so beautiful! She's orange and golden and—but she's having trouble remembering who she is. She needs to see her friends."

Ada and Rowan are already scrambling to their feet. "You mean Marley?" Rowan asks. "She hatched?"

"Not totally. She's still in the middle of it. Oh, come quick!"

"We can't call her Marley anymore," Ada says, sliding her long feet into sneakers, then leaping onto the grassy shelf. "I promised her that. We need to call her something new."